Lujan said, "The Red Death, what's going to happen to California, to America — hell, I have no idea what the world was like before I became a BioStrike trooper."

. . . Hart, too, could hardly remember her former life. Reality for her had become Tucson MedCenter — the elite club formed for those fortunate enough to have escaped the Red Death. "I know what you mean," she told Lujan. "I used to think we were doing the right thing at Tucson MedCenter — keeping our blood pure — but now I'm not so sure."

"You know what I think?" Lujan said, laying her head against the wall of the van and closing her eyes. "The only thing in the world worth stirring an inch for is love. It's sure the only thing worth dying for." She opened her eyes. "I think about dying a lot, Hart. Why not — I won't be Stage One forever. And sometimes . . . I feel like a walking dead woman." She bit her lip. "Even the condemned are entitled to one last wish. But not me. Do you know what my final request would be, Hart?"

Hart shook her head.

Lujan closed her eyes. "To hold a woman in my arms again. To have her hold me. To kiss her."

In The Blood

Lauren Wright Douglas

The Naiad Press, Inc.
1989

Printed in the United States of America
First Edition

Edited by Christi Cassidy
Cover design by Pat Tong and Bonnie Liss
    (Phoenix Graphics)
Typeset by Sandi Stancil

Library of Congress Cataloging-in-Publication Data

Douglas, Lauren Wright, 1947—
    In the blood.

    I. Title
PS3554.0826315 1989   813.54   88-29124
ISBN 0-941483-22-3 (pbk.)

For Martha:
for her help, patience,
unfailing support, confidence,
and honest criticism.

Acknowledgement

I would like to thank Jane M. Orient, M.D., for her help with the ramifications of the Red Death virus, and for her suggestions about future solar technology. I would also like to thank Martha Gilleland, Ph.D., for her assistance with biochemical concepts.

About the Author

Lauren Wright Douglas was born in Canada in 1947. She grew up in a military family and spent part of her childhood in Europe. She began to write poetry and fiction at age nine, and published her first short story at age twelve, in the school newspaper. The thrill of seeing her byline led her to pursue a part-time career in writing, and she has published newspaper articles, essays, poetry, screenplays, short stories, and novels. To support this avocation, she has been a high school English teacher, a newspaper editor, a French translator, a part-time college English teacher, and a public relations writer. She has won several awards for her writing, and recently received a California Arts Council Artist-in-Residence grant to teach short story writing to high school students. Lauren moved to the Southwest in 1983 where she lives with her partner and two cats. *In The Blood* is her third novel, and she has plans to write a sequel.

Books by Lauren Wright Douglas

The Always Anonymous Beast	1987
*Osten's Bay**	1988
In The Blood	1989
Ninth Life	1989 (Forthcoming)

*as Zenobia N. Vole

PROLOGUE

No one is prepared to say when BioStrike actually occurred. All anyone knew was that toward the end of May, 2003, people began to die. It wasn't until October that the Centers for Disease Control began to realize the deaths were exponential, and by then it was far too late to contain the new epidemic. Besides, that winter and spring all of North America was in the grip of the Beijing 'flu — a virus that killed thousands on its own.

So by April of that year, people had more on their minds than recalling a story that had appeared on the

1

six o'clock news programs of Southern California television stations early in December — a story about an explosion that had occurred in the sky over Los Angeles, an explosion that spewed a fine mist into the air. But the mist seemed to do no harm and the story was quickly forgotten.

In actuality the mist did untold harm. The jet stream first carried it south, then east into the highly populated industrialized heartland of the country. As misfortune would have it, it was raining heavily that day. Within twelve hours an estimated twenty percent of the population of the United States had come into contact with the mist.

The cold, rainy spring passed, the Beijing 'flu finally burned itself out, and summer came. But summer brought no respite. On the contrary, it brought something new and terrible. The first deaths attributable to this new disease were reported in Los Angeles in June, and by September over five thousand people had died in Southern California alone. The hospitals were unable to cope — accident victims, coronary patients, even cancer sufferers waited for beds which were never empty.

By fall of 2004, once the C.D.C. admitted that the U.S. had an epidemic on its hands, over half the adults in Southern California were ill. It was then that President Valenzuela delivered his famous "There is no emergency" television address. Meant to reassure, to convince the citizens of America that no unfriendly power had launched a biological strike against them, the address had very little calming effect. It seemed that everyone knew someone who had died or was sick with this new horrible illness. And how else could the

2

epidemic have begun but by a biological strike — BioStrike, as it had come to be called.

But a strike by whom? Serious as they were, these political questions were soon supplanted by concerns of a far more immediate sort. What was this new disease? Was work underway on a vaccine? Was there no cure? The C.D.C. had few answers.

As the epidemic grew in the year following BioStrike, America crumbled. Agribusiness was hit first, and in city after city, food shortages and riots were common. Then the other industries collapsed. Manufacturing, communications, transportation — all important systems shut down as across the country people succumbed to the disease. Those who were still able carried on for awhile, but soon they too simply stopped coming to work. Many locked themselves inside their houses or apartments, believing that they could wait out the disease. There were runs on the banks as people cashed in their life savings and bought guns, ammunition, foodstuffs, blankets, clothes, and over-the-counter medicines.

In a panic, America's creditor nations called their loans. The Federal Reserve Bank, unable to satisfy the lenders, finally closed its doors. Overnight, the American dollar plummeted in value, sending shock waves through the international financial community. The worst selling panic the markets had ever seen took place July 23, 2004, as investments denominated in U.S. dollars quickly became worthless.

In America, hundreds of thousands of people fled the cities for the country; for those left behind, a particularly ghastly hell loomed. Faced with the horror of knowing that their own families, ill with this incurable disease, needed them, the urban police forces *deserted. They went home. Then, with no one to restrain them, gangs of vandals — young people, the homeless, the indigent — trashed and torched the cities in one violent spasm of rage. Radio and television stations, hospitals, schools, factories, banks, corporate offices — symbols of the establishment from which they had been excluded for so long — were raided and burned. Supermarkets, liquor stores, clothing stores were looted. Innocent citizens were murdered by the thousands as gangs fought for dominance. The foreign television crews who attempted to film this carnage were fair game for the looters and vandals. It was as if America was determined to destroy itself in one final paroxysm of violence. And soon, anyone who could fled the country.*

But the exodus was short-lived. As the first refugees crossed the Canadian border only to fall sick and die in Toronto and Vancouver hospitals, it became evident that somehow the disease had to be contained at any cost. In an emergency United Nations session, America's allies — Britain, France, and Israel — led the vote to close America's borders. The logistics alone were daunting. Special U.N. troops manned every Canadian and Mexican border crossing, and turned Americans back. They did the same thing at every international port of entry where American planes might attempt to land or ships to dock. American passengers on the carriers of other nations were immediately quarantined and sent back to their ports of origin. America was sealed tight.

Wrestling with the demands of an unprecedented emergency, Americans fought for survival. They were completely unprepared. The doomsters who had been crying "Disaster!" for decades were finally proven

4

right. As America splintered into regional power units, the survivalists took to the hills. But even then they were unable to defeat the spectre that walked among the survivors, the disease that came to be called the Red Death.

— from notes gathered for *The BioStrike Journals*
by Diana Alfter-Fielding
senior staff writer, *The London Times*
London, England, September, 2007

PART ONE:
ON THE BORDER

CHAPTER 1

"My tongue swore, but my heart was still unpledged."
Euripides, *Medea*

"Here they come," Medina announced, lowering her binoculars. "The train's maybe half an hour away. We should let the others know."

Hart shaded her eyes against the late afternoon sun, and looked out across the desert floor. In the purple haze of distance, just below the mountains, the sun flashed golden on the railway tracks. The train, a sleek black projectile, hurtled toward them with the inevitability of a fired bullet. It disappeared into a tunnel and Hart heard its whistle shriek once, a shrillness that might have been grief. Or pain.

"Damn," Hart swore softly. She turned away from the train to look instead at Medina's strong tanned hands holding the binoculars, at the cascade of silky black hair, at the long straight line of Medina's back under the white coveralls. A wave of longing and resentment washed over her. They had wasted the whole afternoon up here watching for the train, talking about anything other than the topic Hart wanted to discuss: the two of them. And now there was no time left, Hart realized. None at all. "Maybe the train will stall in the tunnel," she said, only half to herself.

Hearing her, Medina pushed her heavy dark hair back behind her ears and looked at Hart reproachfully.

"Oh, I know, I know," Hart said irritably. "You medtechs can't wait to see the Californians."

"It's not as if we're ghouls, you know," Medina objected. "Observing the Californians has a legitimate purpose."

"I know that, too," Hart said, forcing herself to look away from Medina at the jagged tops of the mountains. She knew that the British and Canadians — at the request of the United Nations — were sending a fact-finding mission to America. Or to what was left of America. And because Free Arizona had the lowest incidence of Red Death, the mission was to be based at Tucson MedCenter. "I'm not totally out of it, Medina."

"You sound so bitter," Medina said, reaching over to put a sisterly hand on Hart's shoulder. "Why?"

Hart swallowed, painfully aware of Medina's touch. But she knew, too, that Medina meant nothing by it. This was a gesture she had probably learned from Dr. Ashe. A gesture of compassion. Nothing more. She shrugged Medina's hand away. "Did I sound bitter?" Hart asked. "I didn't intend to. I intended to sound puzzled." She frowned. "Ashe asked me to go, too, you know. But I said no. Any sensible person would say no."

"Why not go? It will make history. Don't you want to be there, Hart?"

"No, I don't," she said honestly. She looked at Medina, wanting to tell her the truth, but afraid of what Medina would think of her if she knew. *I'm frightened, Medina. I've been frightened every day and every night since Dr. Ashe brought me to MedCenter. And I can't stop being frightened.* She shivered. The thought of everyone she knew disappearing into California made her dizzy with panic. But joining them was out of the question. That required courage she didn't have. She simply couldn't do it.

"I'm not going to argue with you," Medina said reasonably. "I'm sure you have your reasons for refusing to go. Just as I have mine for saying yes." She looked steadily at Hart, brown eyes serious. "Hart, you should volunteer for more assignments outside MedCenter. Become more involved with what's going on in the world. Develop a social conscience."

Hart laughed. "Volunteer? Oh no, Medina. Saving the world, or even serving it just isn't in me."

"I don't believe you're as selfish as that," Medina said firmly. "You volunteered for this mission, didn't you?"

Hart shrugged. "I only said I'd come because Dr.

Ashe badgered me about it for two weeks. She said it would be as simple as a drive across Tucson. Besides," Hart said, finally summoning up sufficient courage to look Medina in the eyes, "I had other reasons for coming with the MedTeam."

Medina looked quickly away. "I know," she said. "And I know you want to talk. But I don't think it would serve much purpose. I can't do what you want. I like you, Hart. And I'm happy to be your friend. But anything else . . . And besides, we do have to think about the Intimate Contact Regulations, don't we?"

Hart felt her stomach clench in disappointment. After a moment, when she was able to answer without her voice quavering, she felt her disappointment turn to anger. Medina wasn't being honest with her. "Oh? The Intimate Contact Regulations are academic now, aren't they? After all, we *have* been vaccinated." She looked at Medina accusingly.

Even in the old days, before the discovery of the RD vaccine, it had been possible to circumvent the ICRs. If both partners had clean RD blood workups and were discreet, there was really no problem. And women always had been the lowest-risk RD group anyhow. "What's the real reason, Medina?" she asked.

Medina looked at her sadly. "Oh, Hart. I didn't want to have to get into this. I don't want to hurt you."

"Tell me."

Medina closed her eyes, then opened them slowly, as if in pain. "It's just that you don't seem to . . . to care about anything bigger than yourself. You're all wrapped up in your own concerns. You're like a mole. You pore over your collection of books and tapes of the days before BioStrike. You rebuild antique machinery — all those greasy motors. And whatever time you have left over, you spend with that damned radio of yours, listening to . . . to what? Voices from nowhere. From Sanctuary, supposedly. It's a fairy tale, Hart. A wonderful fairy tale." She took Hart's hands in hers, looking earnestly into her eyes. "It's as if you want to reconstruct the past. To live there. And if you can't live there, then you'll build a fantasy future. Sanctuary is a cruel hoax. You shouldn't waste your energy daydreaming about it." She squeezed Hart's hands. "We'd all like to think there might be someplace we could be safe, someplace life might go on normally again. But for us there isn't. Our world has changed. We only have here and now. We have to live in the present, awful as it is."

Hart was embarrassed by Medina's sincerity, her nearness, the clasp of her hands. She disentangled herself. "Do you think I don't know that?" she said indignantly. "Of course I do."

"Do you?" Medina asked. "If you did, truly, then you'd feel a compulsion to make the world we've been given a better place."

Hart swatted the air. "Why should I have to? Why is all this my responsibility? I didn't cause any of it."

"That's not a helpful response," Medina criticized gently. "Of course we're not responsible for the past. But we are responsible for the future."

Hart groaned. Medina and the other medtechs could argue like this for hours. It was really very simple. Hart wanted nothing to do with the world

13

outside MedCenter; Medina couldn't wait to embrace it.

"You medtechs," Hart said disdainfully. "Do you really think you can beat the Red Death? Save the world?"

"We don't need to save the world," Medina corrected her fussily. "It's only America that's been quarantined. We're the only ones who are sick."

Hart waved away her objection. "But you'll have to cooperate with the Californians. Work with them. It's just too risky. Hell, Medina, no one has even *talked* to a Californian for nearly three years — ever since they closed their borders just after BioStrike."

"Of course it's risky," Medina agreed. "We know that the BioStrike Forces and the Provisional Government are at odds. It's almost like civil war. But we've got something to offer them, Hart. Something concrete. Ashe's vaccine." She continued eagerly, "We know it works. It's still in the experimental stage, but it does the job."

"I know," Hart said wearily. "That's why we're here. To be nice to the Californians. We're supposed to forget their refugees gave us the Red Death in the first place, that we almost starved when they stopped their agricultural shipments to Arizona."

"That's all behind us now. We have to think of the future."

"I am. I'm wondering what they want in return. And why didn't they come to us? What are we doing out here broiling our brains in the sun when they want a favor from *us?*"

Medina raised an eyebrow critically.

Hart held up her hands in surrender. "I know. I ask too many questions. And I worry too much —

about the wrong things. Dr. Ashe tells me that every other day."

"Maybe you should listen to her," Medina said. "I'm sure she'd like you to get more . . . involved in things outside yourself. I'd be flattered if Dr. Ashe took the same interest in me that she's taken in you."

Hart blushed, unable to think of a reply. It was true — Dr. Ashe *did* take an interest in Hart's activities. But Hart, with the same talent she had for keeping everyone at arm's length, had rebuffed Ashe's interest.

"You do seem to worry about the wrong things," Medina observed. "Questions you can't know the answers to. Things you can't change. The past. Wouldn't it make more sense to spend your energy on the present? On making a difference?"

"Like you and Ashe?" Hart said bitterly. "Medina, I can't be like the two of you. And I don't think I care about the wrong things. I care about staying alive. About my future —"

"About your future?" Medina broke in, incredulous. "Hart, if someone doesn't care about *the* future, about this country's future, none of us will live out the decade. That's why I'm going with the British and Canadians to California."

"And that's why I'm not," Hart shot back. "If I'm going to die within the decade, I'm not going to die for a bunch of strangers who mean nothing to me." She jammed her hands into the pockets of her gray coveralls and looked off at the mountains. "I know you probably think I'm denying reality," she told Medina. "I know that's why you won't have anything to do with me. But I can't be any different than I am. I'd like to think I'm not a coward, Medina. But I really don't know." She grimaced. "What I do know is that I'd like the cause to be a little more promising than this one, though."

Medina was silent for a long moment, then she sighed. "We should have talked like this before," she said sadly. "When we first met. Before I started to like you. Oh, Hart, we just see things too differently. I'm afraid we always will."

"I know," Hart said, miserable. And suddenly, there was nothing left to say. "Come on," Hart muttered. "We'd better go tell the others the train is coming."

Medina fell into step with her, and they walked slowly down the little trail to the arroyo where the vans were parked — hers about ten yards away from the other three. All the vans were the same uniform dull gray, but two bore a red cross and TUCSON MEDCENTER in red letters on the side. One was unmarked. Hart's said simply SERVICE.

"You're worried, aren't you?" Medina asked as Hart stopped to pick a handful of jumping cholla needles out of the pant leg of her coveralls.

"You're right about that," Hart said. "Even though we're Free Arizonans and California has no jurisdiction over us, we'll all be crossing the border in an hour or so. Once we're in the Republic of California, anything can happen."

"In theory, yes," Medina agreed. "But remember, they asked for this meeting. They need the Blood Cooling Units. And they need the vaccine."

"I know," Hart told her. "Ashe convinced me that no one else at MedCenter could possibly explain the

16

workings of the solar refrigeration coolers to the
Californians. Even though the units come with their
own manuals, which I wrote. What I don't know,
though, is why half of Tucson MedCenter is here.
Including Dr. Ashe."

Medina shrugged. "We're giving them a hundred
units of RD negative. And the vaccine. I guess Dr.
Ashe wants to explain to them that the virus won't
be affected by transfusions from people who have
been vaccinated."

Hart was skeptical. Everyone knew that once you
had the Red Death, a transfusion would help hold off
the aplastic anemia, but blood from someone who'd
been vaccinated wouldn't cure the disease. "It seems
to me that you or Montalvo could explain that to
them. What a waste of Ashe's time. She's much too
valuable to send off to a dusty border crossing to do
a job any medtech could do. And another thing —
who are those two men riding in the unmarked van?
I've never seen them at MedCenter."

"Someone said they're city supervisors," Medina
said. "But I suppose if I needed to know, I'd know.
And so would you. Oh, Hart, why can't you stop
being so suspicious? If all of us were like you —"
She broke off.

"I know," Hart said sarcastically. "We wouldn't
have any future at all." She looked at Medina for a
long moment, then shook her head. "I'm sorry,
Esther. For all of it."

Clearly startled, Medina looked up at Hart.
"You've never used my first name."

Hart tried to show the sadness she felt. "It's not
encouraged, is it? Since the Red Death started killing

17

us, we've been taught to stay as far away from each other as we can. That's what the ICRs are for, aren't they? Keeping people apart."

* * * * *

Hart jumped down into the dry river bed of the arroyo, brushing off her gray coveralls. Never looking back, Medina had gone ahead to the MedCenter vans, black hair tied back and stuffed up under her white cap. Feeling depressed and abandoned, Hart hurried along the arroyo to the service van.

"You'd better take a look at the solar panels on top of Number Two van," Collins, her driver, called out.

A monkeylike little person, he had a face like tanned leather, and eyes that sparkled mischief. Although he was a man, and Stage One Positive, Hart liked him and always enjoyed working with him. She was sorry that he couldn't live inside the walls of MedCenter as she did, but she understood the need for the regulation — in order to ensure the safety of valuable research and medical personnel, only RD Negatives were allowed inside MedCenter. Hart's spirits rose a little in spite of her gloom.

"I'm going to have a quick look at the dust filters," Collins told her. "It wouldn't do to have a breakdown a hundred yards from the border, now would it?"

Hart grinned. "It would certainly be rotten advertising." She picked up her tool bag and walked over to the cluster of MedCenter vans. Climbing the ladder clamped to the back of Number Two van, she squeezed herself under the solar panels affixed to the

18

vehicle's roof, and began to check them over. The problem was easily located — a loose connection on the fourth panel. She cleaned the connector, blew some dust and grit out of the receptacle, and had the connection reestablished in less than a minute. The red light that indicated POWER ON now glowed reassuringly. She was about to pack up her tools and go when a window was opened in the van beside her.

"Which BioStrike unit is it?" a male voice asked.

"The Sixth," another, deeper male voice answered. An arrogant voice, Hart thought.

"What does Ashe know?" the first voice asked uncertainly.

A low laugh. "Only what they told her at MedCenter — that she's to deliver blood and some samples of the vaccine to one of the BioStrike officers. Nothing more."

"She won't go willingly," the voice warned. "Neither will the MedTeam."

Another laugh. "The BioStrike Unit is commanded by one very tough broad. Probably a dyke, but who cares? She's done this sort of thing before."

"What about the solar tech, and her driver?"

"I don't think they'll be any trouble, but if they are, well, that's their tough luck. They're not our problem. Ashe is. Our job is to get her into the hands of the BioStrike Force. That Provisionary Government they've set up in L.A. is a joke. They wouldn't know what to do with the vaccine even if they had it. The BioStrike Force is the glue that holds that damned state together. Thank God they have enough smarts to realize that once they get their hands on the vaccine, they can stage a military coup. God, we don't care who's in power in California — we just want to

19

be able to deal with them! And if Ashe can't end their epidemic, no one can."

"But will she cooperate?"

"Why wouldn't she? the deep voice said with another laugh. "She's a physician. And a researcher. It'll be irresistible. A chance to play God in California."

"MedCenter considers her a valuable asset," the second voice said fussily. "Will we get her back?"

Silence for a moment. "Probably not. But we don't need her. We have more than enough vaccine. Plus her research notes. And her assistant has assured us he can carry the ball from here. Besides, it's just donkey work now."

"I wish there were another way," the first voice said, sounding regretful. "I find this all very . . . repugnant."

"Oh you do, do you? I'll tell you what I find repugnant. I find the United Nations quarantine of America repugnant. And the oh-so-polite Japanese and Chinese overtures of assistance. And the Alliance of Islamic States' submarines prowling our waters like vultures circling a kill. And the Soviet Union's two-year-old fact-finding mission in Vancouver. Goldman, you know damned well that *we need to have* the quarantine lifted. Thank God the California BioStrike Commander realizes it, too. Those blackshirts are a bunch of maniacs, but I'd make a deal with the devil himself to get that quarantine lifted!"

"All right, all right," the first voice replied. Suddenly the window was closed.

Stunned, unable to move her arms and legs, Hart simply lay there. So her fears had been correct —

20

something other than a fast business deal with the Californians was going on. But this was beyond imagining. They were talking about kidnapping Ashe and Medina. The whole MedTeam, in fact. When she could move again, she crept down the ladder and, heart hammering in her ears, hurried away from the van. She broke into a run, and for an instant wanted to race up the arroyo and into the desert, to run and run and never stop. Calm down, you idiot, she told herself. You've got to do something with this information. Think! Dr. Ashe, her mind supplied. She had to warn Dr. Ashe, tell her what she had heard.

"Where's Dr. Ashe?" she asked, poking her head into an open set of van doors.

Inside, two male medtechs were readying a box of equipment. They looked up at her indifferently. "I dunno," one said. "Gone, I guess."

"Where?"

"Down to the tracks."

"Then where's Medina?"

"With her."

"Oh, hell," Hart answered, slamming the door on the two of them and hurrying away. She stood, hands on her hips, mind racing, desperately trying to think of what to do next.

"I've been looking for you," someone said, coming up behind her, making her jump. Collins pointed back over his shoulder. "Come on. We're leaving."

But I . . . that is, Dr. Ashe —" Hart broke off suddenly, suspicion silencing her. How did she know that Collins wasn't part of this? Caution urged her to say nothing. She'd have to try to warn Dr. Ashe herself, later. "I'm coming," she said warily, following him.

"Say, are you all right?" Collins asked, looking at her in concern.

"Yeah," Hart lied. "Sure. I think I've had a little too much sun, that's all."

"Well, go ahead and stretch out in the back of our van," Collins said kindly. "There's some cool water in one of those containers. Help yourself. We'll drive on down to the border like we were told, but I'd bet my next week's ration coupons that we'll wait there for hours, too."

"Probably," Hart said. She opened the back of the van, tossed her tools in, and crawled in after them. What she had overheard while repairing the van still amazed her. Administrators from Tucson, cooperating with BioStrike Central? Well, why not, she thought cynically. One of the voices had said he'd cooperate with the devil himself to get the quarantine on America lifted.

Hart bit her lip in frustration. Dammit, she didn't want to be involved in any of this. She had only volunteered to come along because Ashe had almost insisted. It would be good for her, Ashe had said. She'd have an opportunity to train technicians. Also, it was an undeniable opportunity to talk to Medina. At MedCenter, Hart never had a chance to talk to her, it seemed. Not only did they work in different departments, but they worked different shifts, and even lived in different parts of the huge complex. Thinking up excuses to run into Medina demanded all Hart's ingenuity. And, really, it had been all for nothing. She shook her head in disgust. Whatever feelings she had for Medina were now doomed because of — what? An ideological difference? "Shit," Hart muttered.

22

Oh come on, she told herself roughly. Why not admit the truth? That you never really expected Medina to return your feelings. That you convinced yourself you cared for her *because* you knew the two of you were ill-matched. That you constructed this elaborate fantasy in order to have someone to think steamy thoughts about. Be honest with yourself: Is Medina really the woman of your dreams?

She sighed, knowing very well the answer was no. As long as she was being honest, she might as well admit that Medina was too prim and proper, too critical, and too self-righteous. She made Hart feel like a misbehaving child.

All at once, she felt a spasm of longing, a desire so keen it hurt. She was usually successful in suppressing feelings, but this one broke the surface of her mind like a diver seeking air. She closed her eyes and, heartsick, allowed herself to want. What did she want? Something simple, of course. Someone she could love. Someone like her own secret self, who wore the face she kept hidden from the world: someone romantic and passionate. Someone who still dreamed. Someone like Suzanna.

Tall, pretty, dark-haired, freckle-faced Suzanna. Hart's childhood friend and adolescent love. They did everything together — climbed trees, collected bugs, read romantic novels to each other, played on the same basketball and volleyball teams. Hart remembered vividly the day Suzanna had told her she loved her. They were in the equipment cupboard at school, pumping up volleyballs after practice when Suzanna carefully closed the door, and came over to Hart, taking the volleyball out of her hands and looking her in the eye.

"I have to tell you something," Suzanna said, fiddling with her braids. "I just figured it out myself."

"What?" Hart had asked, mystified.

"I'm in love with you," Suzanna said. "Like in those books, when the hero suddenly realizes that he doesn't just like the heroine — he loves her. Do you think it's awful?" she asked Hart.

Hart looked at her friend, at the face she had known for twelve years, at the person she loved most in the whole world. "Of course it isn't awful," Hart said hotly. "I feel the same way — I figured it out a few months ago. But you're the one who had the guts to say it."

Suzanna sighed with relief. "It all makes sense now: why I can't stand to be away from you, why I can't imagine being interested in anyone else. Especially not in any of the boys."

Hart felt a huge relief at hearing this. Knowing what she felt, her greatest fear was that Suzanna would suddenly become boy-crazy, abandoning Hart for one of her pimple-faced, smelly male classmates.

"What now?" Suzanna asked Hart. "We're only fourteen. We can't run away and live together. And our parents would die if they found out."

"I don't know," Hart said, miserable. "I guess we go on being . . . best friends. Until we're old enough."

"Okay," Suzanna said.

Suddenly shy, Hart reached over and took Suzanna's hand. "You're more than my best friend, though. I just can't say, you know, that other word."

"I know," Suzanna said. "Neither can I."

Suzanna leaned over and put her lips delicately

against Hart's. "I don't really know how to do this," she whispered, her kiss becoming warmer, more passionate.

"Hey," Hart said shakily, breaking away. "Miss Roberts will catch us for sure."

Suzanna grinned. "She might understand. I have a feeling about her. But you're right — we don't want anyone to catch us. Hey, tomorrow's your birthday — why don't you bring your homework and come over to my house around seven? My parents are going to a movie."

Hart felt as though she would never be able to get a deep breath again, her heart was beating so hard. "Okay," she said, trying her best to sound casual.

But that beginning, that one kiss, was all she and Suzanna had had together. Suzanna's parents didn't go to the movie after all because, quite suddenly, Suzanna's father fell ill. He had just returned from a business trip to Los Angeles. The date was December 13, 2002, one week after BioStrike.

Irritated at her own self-indulgence, Hart closed the door on her feelings. Why long for what you'll never have, she asked herself bitterly. Suzanna is dead. You'll never know anyone that well again, or care that much.

Wiping sweat out of her eyes, she realized how much she wanted to be back in hot, dusty Tucson, to take refuge in the little cubicle where she lived at MedCenter, to return to the safe, dull routine of her job. MedCenter had been her home since BioStrike. Because she was still RD negative, and because, even at fifteen, she had had the rudiments of a skill, a skill she had learned from tinkering in the garage, pestering her engineer father for help with her passion — solar energy technology. She recalled proudly that even at fifteen, she could repair almost any unit, and had earned spending money fixing neighbors' malfunctioning solar hot water panels. Her original designs had won prizes in state science fairs, and once, five hundred dollars in *Solar Energy Times* magazine's annual contest. She smiled, recalling that. But then BioStrike had happened.

Hart sighed. She knew the country couldn't return to the way it had been before BioStrike. Of course it couldn't. She knew as well as anyone that the vaccine was the answer. But kidnapping Dr. Ashe and forcing her to go to BioStrike Central was out of the question. She felt ashamed of Free Arizonan officials for cooperating with this plot. Ashamed and angry. And resentful, too. Why me? she asked herself. Why did I have to be the one to overhear this? I don't want to be a part of it.

She pressed her forehead to her knees, clasping them tightly with her arms. Damn Medina anyhow for accusing her of not caring. Of course she cared. But there were other things she cared about, too. Being safe, for one. And this mission was rapidly unraveling.

But she couldn't stand by and let Ashe be kidnapped, either. Ashe was the person who had saved Hart from the Red Death. Hart shivered, and against her will, she remembered.

For the first six months after BioStrike had occurred, no one realized what was happening, and life continued more or less as usual. Then the six o'clock news began to carry stories of this new disease, and investigative reporters traced its inception

26

back to the explosion in the skies over Los Angeles in December. The media, Hart recalled, coined the phrase "BioStrike." It stuck. Then, suddenly, it seemed that everyone fell ill at once — the teachers at Hart's school, her classmates' parents, her family's neighbors. Almost everyone Hart knew was ill. Then her own parents succumbed. The overburdened Tucson hospitals were unable to cope with the numbers of RD sufferers, so her parents hadn't even bothered to seek medical help. Her father said that the Red Death was worse than the AIDS plague he had lived through in his teens, before there was a vaccine. There was truly nothing medicine could do for this epidemic's sufferers. So her parents decided they would die at home. But the worst part of it was that the stages of the Red Death were by then so well known that her parents were able to count the days remaining to them. Her father grew weaker and weaker, and with his last vestiges of strength, he barricaded the doors and windows, and reminded Hart to take his pistol and ammunition into the fallout shelter with her.

"We can't even kiss you goodbye," he told her that last afternoon, his face disfigured with quarter-sized red blisters. "But never doubt that we love you, Rhiannon. Now go on. Do what I told you to." Tears in his eyes, he turned and walked slowly into the master bedroom. Hart heard the door lock behind him.

"Dad," she whispered, alone in the hall. It didn't seem real. She went on into the kitchen and picked up the pistol and the box of shells her father had left on the table for her. But she was unable to walk to the garage, unable to do what she and her father had discussed. She sat at the table, head in her hands, numbed. And then she heard a curious thing. From the master bedroom, she heard the sound of music. Classical music. Puzzled, she walked quietly back down the hall until she stood outside her parents' bedroom. Yes, it was definitely music. Pachelbel's "Canon," a piece of music her mother loved. It made you think that there was order in the world after all, her mother liked to say. A purpose to things. So the shots, when they came, were particularly sudden and unexpected, and so violent in juxtaposition to this lovely music that Hart was stunned, frozen, the scream lodged in her throat.

"No," she whispered as Pachelbel's chillingly beautiful music cut crystal patterns in the air. "Don't leave me alone!"

But of course, they had.

It was dark when Hart finally managed to go to the garage, release the spring that held the workbench in place, and open the fallout shelter door. No one had been in there for months, and the air was dusty and stale. Somehow, she summoned up enough courage to cross the threshold and seal herself in. And there she stayed, with her bottled water and nitrogen-packed food, for sixty-one days.

Sometimes, when her watch told her it was night, she would cautiously release the shelter's inner door and listen. If she heard nothing, she would then open an observation port in the outer door — a peephole concealed behind a sheet of pegboard — and look out into the garage. If everything seemed safe, she would step out of her hiding place, pistol in hand, walk to the eight-inch barred vertical opening in the wall, and look outside.

At first, gangs of hideous, bleeding, weeping people came to drink out of the fish pond in the front yard. Some stayed for days at a time and, hidden in the darkness of the garage, Hart watched them. The men squabbled and fought over food, clothing, and, she saw in disbelief, the women. Some of them — the ones who had the strength — tried to break into the house, but the wrought iron and her father's barricades kept them out. Then the water in the fish pond dried up, and the people went away. Hart was actually sorry to see them go because then she was truly alone. Except for the dogs. They came out at night, roaming in baying packs, fighting over the dead bodies. One night they smelled her as she watched from the garage window, and four of them gathered, snarling and scratching at the stucco, leaping, slavering, mad to get at her. She had stayed in the shelter after that, too frightened to come out, convinced that the dogs would somehow manage to get into the garage and attack her.

It was only when a clean-up team from Tucson MedCenter had passed through, piling up the corpses for incineration, that she had the courage to come out of the fallout shelter and stand by the window again. She saw the jeeps and heard the helicopter making pass after pass over the golf course behind her house, but she was too frightened to go outside. Then the helicopter left, making a huge circle around the fairway, flying low and heading west. And the jeeps didn't come back. Aghast, she realized that her last hope for rescue had passed. Miserable and hopeless, she slid to the garage floor and put her head on her knees. Huddling there, she thought about crying, but wasn't sure how to start. Then she thought about killing herself, but found to her dismay that she didn't have the courage. She realized she had come to the end of her emotional resources, and she felt nothing save a terrible, black lethargy.

Footsteps on the gravel of her driveway brought her back to reality. Pulling herself up to the window, she looked out. A gray-haired woman with a young face, dressed in white coveralls that said TUCSON MEDCENTER on one breast, looked back at her.

"Jesus!" the woman said. "We were told everyone in this neighborhood was dead."

Hart said nothing. She opened her mouth and tried to respond, but seemed to have lost the power of speech.

"Let me in, honey," the woman urged.

Hart tried to think. "I don't know how," she whispered.

The woman smiled. "Just unlock the garage door and lift it."

Hart did, and with a groaning protest, the door swung up. Daylight flooded in, and through the sunlight strode the woman in white. The light at her back made a halo of her hair, and she seemed to Hart to be a powerful, mystical being. A deliverer. An angel. The angel held out her hand.

"I'm Dr. Ashe," she said.

Hart wiped her palm on the leg of her jeans, then held her hand out to Dr. Ashe. "Rhiannon Hart," she said, intending to be brave. But something — the feel of the doctor's hand in hers, the warmth of her skin, the realization that she wasn't alone after all, destroyed her resolve. Tears began to run down her cheeks, and the more she tried to control herself, the worse it became. "Sorry," she told Ashe in a choked voice.

Ashe put her arms around Hart, and pulled her close. "Go ahead," she told her fiercely. "Cry."

So Hart did. For the first time in sixty-one days she cried. Clinging to Ashe, she wept for her parents, for the life that would now never be hers, and for a world that was dead.

With a start, Hart came back to the present. Yes, she would have to warn Dr. Ashe. Perhaps Ashe could figure out a way to disentangle herself gracefully from the Californians and their expectations before it was too late. And then they'd all go back to Tucson. Which was where they should have stayed anyhow. Hart made a vow to never let herself be talked into leaving the MedCenter compound again. Not even if Dr. Ashe herself asked her. She would refuse. Ashe would have to understand.

Collins started up the van and they bounced over the river bed down to the train tracks. Wedged between two blood cooling units, Hart pillowed her hands under her head and tried to make herself believe that everything would be all right.

* * * * *

Hart peered out through the van's windshield. Against the setting sun, the abandoned train station looked menacing — a blackened skull with broken windows for eye sockets. It was hard to imagine that only ten years ago people had traveled freely between California and Arizona, and had gone calmly about their business here. In the cracked asphalt of the

31

abandoned parking lot weeds now thrived where cars had once parked side by side. A faded sign beside the station proclaimed the name of this border town, but Hart was unable to make it out.

Collins whistled softly.

"What?" she asked. Outside, the sun had set behind the mountains, and suddenly it was twilight.

"BioStrike troopers," Collins said.

Hart felt her palms begin to sweat. In all her years with MedCenter, she couldn't recall anyone's having seen a BioStrike trooper. What she had overheard when she was repairing the solar panel came back to her vividly, and she was suddenly afraid. *Coward,* a sly interior voice accused.

"So soon?" she asked, hoping there was some mistake. "I've got to talk to Dr. Ashe first," she told him anxiously.

"Plenty of time for that later," Collins said, looking at her critically. "Just get your own job done."

"Okay," Hart said, wishing she knew for sure whether she could trust him. Never mind, she'd do this herself. Before any of them got embroiled in their business deals with the Californians, she'd find Ashe and warn her. That couldn't be too hard, could it?

When one of the medtechs knocked on Collins' window, Hart jumped in alarm. He looked in at them with barely concealed impatience, blond brows knit in a frown. Collins rolled down the window.

"Drive right down to the tracks," the tech said. He looked at Hart with unfriendly eyes. Hart knew he envied her home inside the MedCenter compound.

32

As did Collins, and everyone who was RD positive, he lived outside.

"You're supposed to hang your medtag around your neck and wait on this side of the tracks, just opposite the station." Without waiting for an answer, the tech turned and walked away into the dusk, a retreating ghost in his white coveralls.

Collins started the engine, and Hart hunted in her bag for her medtag. She took one quick look at it — encased in plastic, it bore her picture: curly dark red hair, gray eyes, sun-browned skin, and underneath that, her life history, encapsulated:

Name: Hart, Rhiannon S.
DOB: 12/14/1984
Occupation: Solar Technician IV
Blood: Type: O Pos
           RD Status: Class One Negative 04/24/06
           Vaccinated: 10/28/05

She hung the tag around her neck.

"Got the manuals for the cooling units?" Collins asked.

Hart nodded.

"What did you need to tell Dr. Ashe?" he asked. "Anything important? I could do it for you if I see her first."

"No," Hart said. "It was nothing important."

He shut off the engine, and the van coasted to a stop in front of the tracks. Off to the right was the black bulk of the train. Ahead, the deserted station loomed, its shadow a dark shape against the lighter sky.

"Out you go," Collins said.

Hart opened the van's passenger door. Jumping down to the ground, she squared her shoulders and walked with as much dignity as she could muster to the tracks.

All at once, lights went on in the deserted station house. She blinked, momentarily blinded, then she saw in one heart-stopping moment that a dozen BioStrike troopers had lined up in pairs on the California side of the racks. Silhouetted against the station house light, they looked alien, sinister, deadly, lights gleaming off their helmets, faceplates opaque. And they were completely black — black boots, black tight-fitting pants, black jackets, black gloves, and black helmets. The trooper directly across the tracks from her was so close they might have touched if each had stretched out a hand. Now what, Hart wondered, her heart thudding in her throat. As if in answer to her question, one of the troopers snapped on a hand-held light.

"Hold up your medtag," a neutral, tenor voice said. With a start, Hart realized the trooper was a woman.

Hart held the tag out away from her body, and the trooper trained the light on it.

"Look at that — an O positive. And a Red Death Negative Class One, too," she said, plainly surprised. "There aren't many of you Class Ones left. But what were you vaccinated against?"

They really don't know about Ashe's vaccine, Hart realized. My God, how have they survived for so long? "Against the Red Death," she told them, her voice tight.

34

She heard the trooper's muffled exclamation. "Well, well," she said. "So the rumors we hear are true. Come on across, Solar Tech Four Rhiannon S. Hart."

Resentful, giddy with fear, her legs threatening to buckle at the knees, Hard did as she was told.

"Welcome to California," the BioStrike trooper said.

CHAPTER 2

0800 1400 APRIL 2006

FROM: BIOSTRIKE COMMAND, THE PRESIDIO,
     SAN FRANCISCO
TO: 6TH UNIT COMMANDER, LOS ANGELES
CLASS: CONFIDENTIAL///EYES ONLY

*1. You are hereby authorized to deploy the Sixth
Unit personnel to detain and secure the persons of Dr.
Jean Ashe, the accompanying Tucson MedCenter team,*

and, as required, any other Free Arizonans you deem
necessary to the success of this mission.

2. You are reminded that the BioStrike Force
under your command acts with full military authority.
As such, you are authorized, and indeed required, to
enforce the BioStrike Edicts before your return to Los
Angeles. Personnel under your command are to assist
in the confiscation and/or disposal of contraband or
quarantined materials. Relevant provisions regarding
these items and materials can be found in DOD
6877.12.

3. This order shall remain in effect until you are
debriefed.

* * * * *

Captain Zia Sandoval woke with tears on her face.
Swinging her legs off her cot and fumbling in the
dark for her watch, she snapped on the light and
checked the time — nearly seven o'clock. Running
water into a little basin, she washed her face, then
combed her hair with her fingers and looked quickly
in the mirror. A dark, brooding face looked back at
her, lips drawn in a grim line, brown eyes cynical,
one eyebrow permanently raised in disenchantment.
Her face looked gaunt, she thought, the cheekbones
too sharply prominent. She knew she was too thin,
but lately she had had no interest in food. It was as
if some part of her had decided that she should be
made smaller, perhaps to present a less tempting
target to a hostile world. You're burning yourself out,

37

Zia, her reflection said to her. This has to stop. She laid her head against the cool glass of the mirror. I know, she told herself. I know.

And she had had her recurring dream of childhood again — a haunting, poignant time capsule of the last happy time in her life. Damn it, anyway. Carefully, she let the water out of the little basin, folded her towel, put away her soap, and straightened the covers of her cot. Smoothing the wrinkles out of her black pants, she made certain that her shirt was tucked in all the way around, then reached for her weapons belt. The bloody thing must weigh five kilos, she thought wryly, settling it into position on her hips. Donning her black leather jacket, she picked up her helmet and opened the door of the railroad command car.

Stepping down from the train into the cool dark of the desert night, she shivered a little, zipping her jacket higher. She ran a hand through her hair once more, noting in irritation that it was definitely too long. She'd have to get it cut soon, or BioStrike Central's spy, the punctilious Lieutenant Valentin, would pass one of her seemingly casual comments about it. And then write furiously in the little black notebook which she kept in her left-hand breast pocket. Sandoval snorted again. Well, let her write.

Sandoval stretched until her shoulder joints popped. Valentin. Trust BioStrike Central to have saddled her with such a creature. Not that Sandoval minded having a spy to contend with — hell, she'd had them before — but this one was barely human. In fact, two weeks ago, she had literally dropped out of the sky. Strapped into that infernal machine she called the SunRaycer, Valentin had floated down just

38

in front of the engine car, landing the vehicle squarely on the tracks ahead of the stationary train. She had startled the train's engineer, Corporal Villanova, so badly that the trooper came within a whisker of turning her M-22 on the SunRaycer, thereby sending Valentin to the apocalyptic end she so richly deserved.

Sandoval frowned, leaning against the command car, thinking about Valentin. She had seen Valentin's ilk before — years before — when she had been, for a mercifully short period of time, a BioStrike recruiter. She'd seen plenty of Valentins. And she had always rejected them as unfit for service — her own feeble protest against a system that was, in reality, tailor-made for those exactly like Valentin. For those with a talent for lies and stealth, for the mean-spirited cowards, the sadistic bullies. Finally, Sandoval's actions had caught up with her, and she had been banished to the front lines. For the past three years she had been in command of the Sixth BioStrike Unit. The Kidnap and Murder Squad. Sandoval twisted her lips in a bitter smile. It was a sobriquet which brutally reflected the truth.

Raising her face to the sky, she searched for the evening star. There — just above the horizon. Venus. It pleased her to be able to name things, and she knew the pleasure came from a small measure of control over a world run amok. She marveled at how clearly the stars shone, and how close they seemed — as if, were she to raise a hand, they would be at her fingertips.

Thinking she heard a rustle in the inky darkness between the train's cars, she froze, hand on her sidearm.

39

"Identify yourself," she demanded quietly.

Another rustle, and then a lizard ran over the tops of her boots, pausing for one heartbeat to look up at her, moonlight reflecting from its jeweled eyes. She relaxed.

Looking down the tracks at the station house, and her troopers deployed in neat pairs along the train's length, she decided to stay here, hidden, for just a few more moments. Hardly breathing, eyes closed, she leaned back against the train. She heard voices at a distance, faintly, but here, in this bubble of silent, dark isolation, it was possible to believe herself alone.

I'm so tired, she thought. How much more of this can I take — can we all take? We're nothing more than cannon fodder, bodies to be thrown against the advancing tide of the Red Death. If it weren't for us, she thought grimly, and our government-sanctioned "adventures" across California's borders in search of RD negative blood, that damned Provisional Government would have come crashing down long ago. We literally provide the lifeblood that keeps things going. Well, maybe this will be the end of it. Maybe this Dr. Ashe and her vaccine really will make a difference.

She fingered the medtag clipped to the breast pocket of her jacket. So far she was RD negative. But several of her troopers were Stage One Positives, and they were due to be transfused at the end of the month. Flores, Villanova, and Lujan. That left them exactly five days to get back to Los Angeles. Or to an Assessment and Treatment facility. A slim margin of safety, but a workable one.

"Captain Sandoval?" a voice called softly.

"Yes, Corporal Lujan." She stepped out from

40

between the cars, startling Lujan. The young corporal had her gun out of her holster and in her hand before Sandoval could speak, but she reholstered the weapon when she saw who it was. Her helmet under one arm, Lujan came to attention. In the light from the station house, Sandoval could see the lines of weariness and disillusionment on the intelligent young face. She felt a pang of pity — Lujan had been with her for most of the three years she had been on border duty. The difference was that Lujan was nineteen, Sandoval past forty. This despicable duty had been Lujan's only professional life experience as a free woman. Well, almost free, Sandoval amended.

Sandoval recalled very well the day, three years ago, when she had met Lujan at the women's holding facility outside Los Angeles. Lujan was a troublemaker, the officials had told Sandoval. A thief, an arsonist, and probably a murderer on the outside, and here at the prison she was running true to form. She was a good-for-nothing rabble rouser. Sandoval learned that the young woman had half the facility in debt to her for favors done by the other half, and was well on her way to climbing to the top of the power structure.

Sandoval smiled at the memory. She had liked Lujan immensely from the moment she had seen her. A tough, cocky little Chicana, she had looked Sandoval up and down, and finally decided that she would hear what the BioStrike captain had to say.

"I don't want to join no army," Lujan had told her belligerently. "I'd knife the first man who tried to get into my pants. I don't *like* men."

"Is that it?" Sandoval had asked her.

"Huh?"

"Is that your only objection to becoming a BioStrike trooper?"

Lujan had blinked furiously. "Well . . . yeah."

"Fine," Sandoval said. "Because you won't be going to a regular unit. You'll be going to the Sixth. To the unit I'm going to command. They're all women. I'm picking them."

Lujan's mouth had almost fallen open. "They are?" She began to grin.

Sandoval killed the grin with a glare. "The Sixth is the toughest BioStrike unit. It operates on the border. Do you know its nickname?"

Lujan shook her head.

"The Kidnap and Murder Squad. They say that to our faces. Do you know what they call us behind our backs?"

"What?"

"Vampires."

"Why?"

"Because the Sixth crosses the California border to steal blood, Lujan. RD negative blood. The blood of the very young and the very old, of nuns and lesbians. Pure blood. Blood that's still in its containers."

Lujan understood at once. "People," she told Sandoval. "The Sixth kidnaps people." She looked down at the floor. "It sounds pretty much like what I was doing before I came here." She looked up, and Sandoval could see that she wasn't trying to make a joke. She was absolutely serious. And Sandoval saw something else, too — something fierce, bright, and strong, something that lived behind Lujan's eyes, something that deserved its chance. She decided she'd give Lujan that chance.

"You don't have the Red Death, do you?"

Lujan shook her head, clearly insulted. "No way."

Sandoval was skeptical. "In a place like this, how did you avoid it?"

Lujan crossed her arms over her breasts and looked at Sandoval flatly. "My . . . girlfriends and I look out for each other. It's the women who fuck around with the men guards — they're the ones who get it." She shrugged. "Knowing how not to get the Red Death is the easy part. The hard part is doing it. The women who get sick, well, some of them are loners. They can't make the guards leave them alone. Other women think that fucking the guards will get them privileges." She laughed bitterly. "All it's gotten them is a death sentence. No, we let the men know we weren't going to play with them. We had to cut a few who didn't believe us, but they learned pretty soon to stay away."

Sandoval was impressed. "I'll see you in six weeks," she told Lujan, handing her a copy of the form she had been filling out. "You'll be a private. Then, if things work out, a corporal. You'll be under my command. We're going to the Sixth, Lujan. We're going to be fighters." When this didn't seem to deter the young woman, Sandoval told her, "We're going to fight the Red Death."

Lujan watched her, unmoved. "Well, will we beat it?" she asked. "I don't like to lose my fights."

Sandoval looked into the shrewd brown eyes, and decided this was the woman she would choose as her aide. "No," she told her, "we won't beat it. We've never beaten it. The Red Death is really nothing more than an old enemy come round in new clothes."

She smiled at Lujan. "You don't know about the Four Horsemen, do you?"

Lujan shook her head.

"I'll tell you," Sandoval said. "It's a story we should all know. The Four Horsemen of the Apocalypse are characters in the Revelations of St. John the Divine. They are supposed to herald the end of the world. The first will be Conquest, on a white horse; the second, War, on a blood-red horse; the third, Famine, on a black horse."

"And the fourth?"

"The fourth will be Death," Sandoval said.

Lujan looked back at her, unafraid.

"Do you still want to come to the Sixth, Lujan? You'll get to see the Fourth Horseman, I can guarantee that."

Without hesitation, Lujan nodded.

"Do you have any questions?"

"Only one," Lujan said, folding the form Sandoval handed her and putting it in her pocket. "What do I call you?"

Sandoval decided a smile wouldn't hurt anything. "Sandoval," she said. "Captain Sandoval. Or just Captain. Don't worry. At Central, they'll teach you military etiquette. I imagine you already know the rest."

* * * * *

Remembering, Sandoval smiled again. That was a good memory. But with a start, she came back to the present. Someone had been calling her. "I'm here," she told Lujan, wondering what the young corporal thought. Well, it wasn't the first time Lujan had stumbled over her brooding in the dark.

"Everything's ready, Ma'am," Lujan said, saluting.

"Report," Sandoval said crisply.

"Yes, Ma'am," Lujan said. "The purchase of the blood cooling units from the Free Arizonans is underway in the station house. Private Flores is in command of that detail. The donors — those women who call themselves Gaians — are being allowed to leave the train to wash and eat. Corporal Villanova is in charge."

"Very good," Sandoval said. "Where are they?"

"Who, Ma'am?"

"Our enforced guests. Los Angeles' newest blood donors. The followers of Gaia." Try as she might, she was unable to keep the sarcasm out of her voice.

"About a hundred yards from the train," Lujan said, pointing out into the night. "There's a little hill between us and them. They're just on the other side."

"All right," Sandoval said. "And the third detail?"

"As you ordered, Ma'am, Private de la Rosa is coordinating it."

"Fine, Corporal," Sandoval told her. "I'd like to observe de la Rosa. Walk with me, Lujan." She put on her helmet, but flipped the visor up. Lujan did the same. The two women each pulled out a hand-held light, and broad beams of yellow lanced ahead of them, picking out a winding trail lined with shoulder-high jumping cholla and clumps of desert broom.

It's been a long time, she thought, inhaling greedily. A little breeze brought a spicy odor to her nostrils, and she smiled in satisfaction that she remembered its name, too: desert creosote. It's spring, she realized with a pang of regret. Another spring. Another year gone.

"Did you ever get any sense out of the Gaians?" Sandoval asked. "I know you intended to question them. What did they say?"

Lujan laughed. "I'm not sure. They're servants of the earth, or some such thing. Keepers of the blood. Also — and one of the women let this slip — they're in touch with a network of women like themselves who are all bound for some kind of haven where they intend to ride out this pestilence that has claimed the earth. Those are their words, Captain, not mine."

"A haven?" Sandoval scoffed. "Where is it? I'm sure BioStrike Central would like to know about it."

"Of course, they wouldn't tell *me*," Lujan said. "It was the crazy woman who mentioned it. Sanctuary, they call it."

"Sanctuary?"

"That safe place where they're going to wait for the Red Death to pass."

Sandoval laughed. "How fitting that a crazy woman told you this. Haven't we been searching for one form of Sanctuary or another for centuries?" She laughed again. "I'll have to talk to those women myself. Who's the leader?"

"An Indian woman named Onava. She . . ." Lujan hesitated.

"Yes?"

"She has . . . secrets in her eyes," Lujan said at last. "I can't explain it any other way."

"A lovely phrase," she said quietly. Ah, Lujan, she thought sadly. We've wasted you. Thrown you away.

They walked on, Sandoval thinking about Lujan's comment. Every once in a while Lujan said something so perceptive, so poetic, that it made Sandoval's heart turn over. Suddenly she felt the need to offer Lujan something in return. Something private.

"Do you know that I was born here, Lujan?"

"Here, Ma'am?" Lujan asked, surprised.

"Well, not in this precise spot," Sandoval said wryly. "But in the high desert. In a little town just east and north of here. My father had what used to be called a dude ranch. He named it Carefree. I thought it was paradise. The nights smelled just like this."

"Carefree is a fine name," Lujan answered diplomatically.

"It's a foolish name," Sandoval said softly. "My father was a poet, not a businessman. Really, Lujan, you're too indulgent. But it makes a pleasant memory. Tell me, Corporal, where's your home? I don't believe I know where you were born."

"East Los Angeles, Ma'am. I never lived anywhere else."

"God," Sandoval said, appalled.

"Oh, it wasn't so bad," Lujan offered. "I didn't know anything different. I used to see other places on TV or at the movies, but they might as well have been on the moon."

Sandoval frowned. She didn't like Lujan's tone of resignation. Did the young woman think this was the end of the line for her? Sandoval half wished she could ask. "I've been thinking of requesting a promotion for you, Lujan. And a transfer."

"A transfer?" Lujan replied, clearly surprised.

"Where, Ma'am?" Sandoval noted that she seemed unimpressed at the prospect of promotion.

"I thought San Francisco, Lujan. Or Monterey. Someplace pretty. And someplace far away from all this border action."

"But Captain, I . . . All this border action — doesn't someone have to do it?"

I'm not sure anymore, Sandoval wanted to say. Instead, she took refuge in evasion and military double-talk. "Of course, corporal. But you've done more than your duty."

"Well, I . . . that is, I . . ." Lujan trailed off. Sandoval heard her take a deep breath, as if coming to a difficult decision. "Captain, may I speak freely?"

Sandoval was mystified. "Yes, certainly. Go ahead."

"I'd like to stay with you, Ma'am."

Sandoval couldn't have been more amazed had Lujan declared she wanted to sprout wings and flap back to Los Angeles. "Such loyalty is commendable in one so young," she said, careful to keep any trace of sarcasm from her voice. She was more touched than she liked to admit. "And in return I'll speak freely to you. Listen to me now."

"Yes, Captain," Lujan whispered.

"All hell is going to break loose in California. Soon. You've heard — we've all heard — that BioStrike command is changing. That the old guard, the officers who supported the Provisional Government, are on the way out. Something's happening, Lujan. Something big. There's even been talk of California opening its borders again. But that can't happen while the present government is in power. Or while units like the Sixth are in operation. We'd be an embarrassment to the new government. They wouldn't want to admit what's been going on here for the past three years. Lujan," she said quietly, "the Sixth — our BioStrike Unit — is going to take the brunt for the Provisional Government's ill-conceived plans to curb the Red Death. We'll be their scapegoats. I don't know anything more, but that's probably enough. I can promote you right here, and write your transfer papers, if necessary. I advise you to take them, and run as fast as you can to a nice safe posting. I can't do much to reward your loyalty. But I can do that."

Lujan said nothing, and Sandoval thought she should sound one final urgent note.

"But make your mind up soon, Lujan. I don't know how much longer I'll be here."

"It's that damned Lieutenant Valentin," Lujan said vehemently.

"Yes, minus the adjective," Sandoval agreed. "She's a member of the new order. The new elite. I suspect Valentin will report that I'm no longer fit to command."

"That's crazy!" Lujan exploded. "No one else could have saved our asses the way you have!"

Sandoval grinned. "I thank you, Corporal, but as Lieutenant Valentin will discover, I do have one fatal flaw. And it's becoming more pronounced as I grow older. It's worse than a flaw — it's a disability, in fact."

"A disability?" Lujan said in disbelief.

I can no longer send those I love to die, Sandoval answered mentally. For Lujan's benefit, however, she

49

said aloud, "I'm no longer willing to take risks," she told her corporal. "Valentin sees it as something different. But she sees it nonetheless."

Lujan snorted derisively, but said nothing.

They walked side by side in silence until they approached the station. Sandoval put a hand on Lujan's arm. "Lights out," she said. "We'll just wait here on the platform and see how de la Rosa handles things." She climbed the cracked concrete steps, Lujan close behind. "Over here," she said. "We have a good view of the Arizonans' vans. Let me have your night glasses."

Seen through the starlight lenses, the scene at the Arizonans' vans could have been taking place in bright daylight. De la Rosa and two BioStrike troopers were shaking the Arizonans' hands and pointing back toward the train. In a moment the whole party — Sandoval's troopers and the Arizona medtechs — began to move in the direction of the train. "Take a look," Sandoval said. "It seems de la Rosa has quite a touch. They're walking right into our arms."

"They are, Ma'am," Lujan said. "Quite a difference from that action last month."

"Quite," Sandoval agreed sadly, remembering the dead.

"Captain!" Lujan whispered suddenly. "Who's that?"

Sandoval turned. A small figure in gray coveralls was standing in the shadows beside the ruined station house. One of the Arizonans, she guessed. She heard the creak of leather as Lujan drew her pistol, and she put a hand on the other woman's arm to restrain

50

her. "Don't shoot her unless you have to," Sandoval said.

Lujan murmured agreement.

The Arizonan stepped to the edge of the platform. Just below her, and about ten yards to her left, de la Rosa was leading the medtechs across the tracks and around the front of the train.

As Sandoval watched, the figure hesitated, seemed to come to a decision, then stepped back into the shadows, shoulders slumped. Puzzled, Sandoval motioned Lujan forward. "Let's see what this is all about," she said quietly.

Back turned, the figure was watching de la Rosa and her troopers lead the Arizonans into one of the railway cars. Lujan and Sandoval came within ten feet of her before she heard them and whirled, startled. It was a young woman, Sandoval saw, about Lujan's age, but smaller and slimmer. Maybe five feet four. Red hair, tanned face. The young woman faced Sandoval, fists clenched.

"Are you in charge here?" she said.

Amused, Sandoval held up a hand to restrain Lujan. She answered, "I am."

"Then let them go! You have no right to do this."

"Maybe not," Sandoval said sadly. "But I have the power. That's what counts these days, isn't it?"

The Arizonan said nothing, but they were so close that Sandoval saw her lower lip begin to tremble.

"You must be the solar tech," Sandoval said. "I have no orders concerning you. At least, no direct orders. I advise you to go back to Arizona while you still can."

51

The young woman blinked, stood up very straight, then reached for the front of her coveralls.

"Keep your hands where I can see them!" Lujan called, stepping out from behind Sandoval.

The Arizonan blinked again, tears of anger and determination in her eyes. Sandoval felt the buzz of tension in the air, and her stomach tightened. Ignoring Lujan's warning, the young woman thrust a hand into her pocket where something bulky rested.

Dammit, Sandoval thought, she's got a gun.

"This is for you," the Arizonan said in a choked voice.

It was on the tip of Sandoval's tongue to try and talk her out of such rashness, to urge her to be sensible, to say something to make her turn and walk away, when she heard the unmistakable *ssst* of Lujan's pistol. The young woman screamed, stumbled sideways, and dropped to the concrete. Something heavy fell from her pocket and skittered across the platform to Sandoval's booted feet. Sandoval prodded it, turning it over. It seemed to be a book of some kind. She knelt, retrieved it, and held it up to the light. *A Manual for the Maintenance of Solar Refrigeration Cooling Devices,* the cover said. *Written for the California BioStrike Forces by Rhiannon S. Hart.*

CHAPTER 3

Nature is trying very hard to make us succeed,
but nature does not depend on us. We are not
the only experiment.

Buckminster Fuller
Spaceship Earth

A raging thirst awakened Hart. Groggy, she
reached for the bottle of water she always kept on
the shelf above her bed in the dorm at Tucson
MedCenter. But this morning it wasn't there. Nor, for

that matter was the shelf. Half asleep, she tried to orient herself. Where was she?

She opened her eyes. In the dim light she could barely make out the rough grain of a plank wall, not more than six inches from her nose. But it suggested nothing to her. She ran her hands over the hard surface she lay upon, seeking an answer there. It, too, was unfamiliar. She turned onto her back, surprised at how ill and tired she felt. I'll get up in a minute, she told herself. I'll remember then. Everything will be all right.

She closed her eyes for a moment and when she opened them again a face appeared in front of hers. Before she could check her reaction, she cried aloud, so grotesque was this apparition. It was a woman, an old woman whose long gray hair, staring, red-rimmed eyes, and toothless mouth gave her the appearance of a witch. Or a madwoman. The woman reached out to touch Hart's hair, and Hart flinched away from her clawlike hand.

"Hair on fire," the woman crooned rocking back on her heels.

With a stab of horror, Hart realized that this witchlike woman really wasn't old at all. She swallowed. What could have happened to her?

Suddenly memory flooded back, and she shut her eyes tight. *Coward,* a mocking inner voice accused her. You couldn't even speak up to warn Dr. Ashe. You let her walk right into the Californians' trap because you were too frightened to call out to her.

"So you're awake," a voice said quietly from behind her head.

Hart turned. A brown-eyed woman with curly pale

hair knelt to put a candle down on the floor between them.

"Don't mind Irena," the brown-eyed woman told Hart. "She's harmless."

"'What's . . . what happened to her?" Hart asked looking over at the bundle of rags that was Irena.

The woman shrugged. "We're not sure." She looked at Hart critically. "Can you walk?"

"I don't know," Hart said. She got her legs under her and prepared to stand.

"Here," the woman said, holding out a hand to help her.

Hart took it and with the woman's help, she stood. Immediately, she regretted it. Leaning back against the wall, she closed her eyes. "Give me a minute," she said weakly. "I feel a little sick." She tried to open her eyes, but it was just too much trouble. "What's the matter with me?" she asked, swallowing with difficulty, remembering her thirst. "Do you have any water?"

"Yes, of course," the woman said.

"We'll take her, Cora," a new voice said.

Hart opened her eyes. "Take me where?" she asked, looking around apprehensively. "Where am I, anyhow?"

A very tall woman studied Hart. A mystic, Hart thought — large, expressive brown eyes, flowing dark hair, an other-worldly demeanor. But then Hart saw the sensible boots, the long, heavy blue cotton skirt with pockets, the tan workshirt. A practical mystic, Hart amended. But those eyes. So dark they seemed black, they caught Hart's eyes and held them. After a moment of suffering the other woman's study, Hart realized she could bear no more of this. It was as if her soul was being peeled like an onion. In a moment of panic, she wrenched her gaze from the woman's eyes. She had no desire to bare her soul to anyone, and least of all to this stranger. "You're here with the rest of us on the BioStrike trooper's train," the woman said quietly. "We haven't pulled out yet."

"Pulled out?"

"Left."

"I don't understand," Hart said. "Left for where?"

The woman's lips turned up in what might have been a smile on another face. On hers it was an expression of regret. "Los Angeles."

Hart remembered suddenly, and clutched her shoulder as her body relived the pain of having been shot. But, amazingly, there was no wound. The tall woman looked at her impassively.

"They *shot* me!" Hart said. "Why . . ."

A soft giggle rose from Irena, the madwoman. "Los Angeles," she said in wonder. "We'll surely see the angels there." She cocked her head and looked up at Hart. "But look — one's here already," she said, examining Hart with a fierce concentration Hart found daunting. "Hair-on-fire," she said querulously. "Are you the one? I can't be sure. Oh, go away, angel. You'll just cause us sorrow."

To her surprise, Hart saw that the women were actually listening gravely to Irena's babbling. Dismayed, she felt the need to speak. "I'm no angel of death," she said. "I was grabbed when the BioStrike troopers took the other Arizonans."

"Not quite," Cora said skeptically. "The BioStrike troopers dumped you in here a couple of hours ago.

56

They had you all last night and today. We wonder what they did with you."

"Vampires," Irena said decisively, hugging herself. "They gave her to the vampires."

Cora looked at Hart's medtag. "If you're RD negative, you're fair game. You're O positive, too. And look at that!" she whistled. "Vaccinated. Is this the famous Ashe vaccine we've been hearing about?"

Hart nodded. "Yes. But where did you hear about it?"

As if she had said too much, Cora fell silent.

"In the ether," Irena told Hart. "Where the angels fly."

Hart shook her head. It occurred to her that perhaps all the women here were mad. It was not an encouraging prospect.

"Oh, we know why you're here," Irena told Hart. "That blackshirt devil commander put you in here with us to find out about Sanctuary. First she sent the young black ferret. And now a clever red fox. She —"

"That's enough, Irena," Cora said, patting her arm.

"Come and sit with us, Arizonan," the tall woman offered.

Hart hesitated for a moment. All her instincts told her to find the way out of here, then run. But her common sense told her to wait. She might learn something useful from these women. "All right," she said, hoping soon to make sense of all this. It seemed a scene from a dream. Or a nightmare. The tall woman moved aside and Hart looked past Cora and Irena. A quartet of women stood just behind Irena, shoulder to shoulder, blocking Hart's view of the rest of the car. Hart looked them over. One of them was a small, muscular woman, her hair braided, one hand jammed into the pocket of a pair of worn black pants, a once-white shirt rolled up to her elbows.

"You asked for water," she said sharply, holding out a battered aluminum cup.

Hart looked at the woman cautiously, then took the cup and emptied it in a single gulp. Nothing had ever tasted so good, she thought. "Thank you. Is there more?"

The woman shrugged. "Some. Over there."

She turned away from Hart, and Hart tried her best to control her anger. *Listen,* she said silently to the woman, *whatever's been done to you hasn't been done by me. I'm getting a little tired of all these foul looks.*

The four women opened ranks to let Hart and the tall woman through. Hart took a step forward, and when she was able to see clearly what the railway car contained, she frowned. Women sitting in groups of three, or four, or five, huddled around candles that burned in cups or jars on the floor. Hart counted at least half a dozen such groups.

"Who are all these women?" Hart asked, feeling her skin prickle.

The woman with the braided hair looked at the tall woman, then back at Hart. "Donors," she said, her voice flat.

"Donors? Whose donors? I didn't know there was a MedCenter near here."

The tall woman looked her over, then motioned for her to sit down. Hart did so, and the others joined her, forming a circle around the candle. They were silent, and Hart realized they were waiting for

58

someone to speak. She looked from face to face, and realized that the tall woman was the one they were waiting for. The leader. All right, Hart thought. This is the person I have to deal with. She turned her attention to her.

"You seem to be an innocent," the tall woman said. "And maybe you truly are." She hesitated a moment, then held her hand out across the circle. "My name is Onava."

Hart was surprised. That was an Indian name — yet the woman didn't look Indian at all. "That's an O'odham name," Hart said tactfully. "The Sonoran desert people. Are you from Arizona?"

"At one time, yes," the woman said.

Hart waited, but no further information was offered. She shrugged, and extended her own hand to Onava. But Irena, seated beside her, reached out one bony claw and grabbed her wrist. With surprising strength she held onto Hart while her other hand peeled back Hart's sleeve. "Look!" she said. "Vampire tracks!"

Hart looked down in horror. A small, neat bandage was in place over the vein in the crook of her arm. It was suddenly clear to her what the BioStrike troopers had done to her, and why she couldn't remember anything — they had drugged her and used her as a donor. She felt sickened and enraged.

So the unpleasant names given to the BioStrike troopers were correct after all: they *were* bloodsuckers, vampires, blood-buyers. She shivered. And if the names were, after all, right, what of the stories Hart had heard? Could it be possible that the BioStrike troopers really did steal children? That they maintained secret camps of people who were RD negative, raising them like cattle for their blood? That they raided across the borders, seeking out enclaves of individuals who kept their blood pure — particularly groups of far-sighted women who had been clever enough to run and hide immediately following BioStrike?

Irena prodded the bandage. "Vampires," she said fearfully.

Someone reached to comfort Irena, and the madwoman sobbed gently in the woman's arms.

"You must forgive her," Onava said. "She was like that when we found her. We think she had been used as a donor in one of the Californians' more unscrupulous blood camps. It's just as well she has taken refuge in madness."

"They used me as a donor," Hart said in disbelief. "They drugged me. And they probably took too much blood. That's why I'm so weak."

Onava nodded. "Quite likely."

Hart looked across the circle at her, realizing the ritual of introduction had been interrupted. "I'm Hart," she said, extending her hand.

Onava took it, and Hart was surprised at the other woman's warmth. Her own hand felt like a block of ice in the woman's warm grasp.

Someone poured Hart more water from a plastic jug, and handed it around the circle. Hart took the water gratefully.

"Hart is a strange name," Onava said. She looked directly at Hart, and Hart looked up once, quickly. But Onava's eyes were shuttered now. Ebony mirrors.

"It's my surname," Hart told her. "We've used surnames ever since BioStrike. I've gotten used to it."

60

Hart looked around. "Who are all these women? What's going on?"

Onava gave her a long, searching look.

"You don't really think I'm a spy, do you?" Hart said in amazement.

One of the other women spoke up, a small dark woman in a brown shirt and pants. "I'm Eda. And yes, some of us wonder about that."

"They *shot* me," Hart told her.

"No," Eda corrected her. "We heard the guards talking. It seems that the blackshirts only tasered you."

"What?"

"They used a taser. A gun that fires electricity instead of bullets."

"Oh," Hart said. That would account for what she had felt — one excruciating moment of pain in which it seemed that a million volts of electricity had passed through her body. She had read about such weapons. "But I thought a taser had to be applied directly to the skin," she said.

"Not this version," Eda said. "The BioStrike troopers must be getting arms from outside the country. Some of their weapons are pretty sophisticated." She looked pointedly at Hart.

"I'm not one of them, damn it. I'm an Arizonan — a solar tech. I came with the Tucson MedCenter team. I overheard that the Californians intended to kidnap the medtechs and Dr. Ashe. I wanted to warm them. They caught me."

"So we heard," Eda said. "But why did they keep you for a whole day?"

"I don't know," Hart said wearily. "You tell me."

"Enough, Eda," Onava said firmly. "Harassing

Hart will do no good. She's one of us now it seems, no matter what was done to her."

"Oh no," Hart objected, her skin crawling. "I won't be anyone's donor! And I'm damned well not going to Los Angeles."

Onava looked at her as one would a child, and Hart bristled. She reminded herself again to control her anger. Right now she needed information. "How did you fall into the BioStrike troopers' hands?"

"They came in the night and rounded us up," Eda told her.

"I don't understand," Hart said. "You can't just round people up like so many cattle."

"Of course you can," Onava said matter-of-factly. "The way your fellow Arizonans were taken is proof of that. A superior force makes retaliation useless."

"You mean you didn't resist?" Hart asked, stunned.

"It's not our way," Onava explained. "Three years ago, after BioStrike, we decided to retreat into the hills to try to live in peace and harmony with nature. We took an oath to the earth, to Gaia. We vowed to keep ourselves apart. It was possible, we felt, that we might eventually be the only survivors of this devastating disease. We decided to wait it out. If humankind won, and the disease abated, we'd rejoin the mainstream of life. If the disease won, then it would be a sign from Gaia."

"From Gaia? Who's Gaia?"

Onava looked at Hart in gentle reproach. "The Earth. Or, if you prefer, the Goddess. They are one, after all."

Hart thought she understood about Gaia. But this

62

business of the sign confused her. "What kind of sign?"

"A sign that the stewardship of the earth was to pass into our hands."

Hart was skeptical. "But if you believe this — that Gaia might intend you to be stewards of the earth — why did you let the BioStrike troopers take you? Why didn't you fight to stay free? Surely you can only do this if you're free."

"Fighting never solved anything," one of the women said decisively.

"Fighting got us BioStrike," another agreed.

Hart shook her head. These answers made no sense. What sort of people wouldn't fight to stay free? People who didn't value freedom very much, she guessed. People like Onava. And what was worse, the women's answers had the feel of rote about them — something memorized, and now repeated. "But if you don't fight — and it's not too late to do it even now — you might not be alive to claim your stewardship. Then what?"

Onava shrugged. "Then clearly Gaia doesn't need us. We can't know her plan. Perhaps she intends to remove all vestiges of humanity from herself. To cleanse herself. We have caused her only harm, after all. Perhaps humanity has had its chance."

"Or perhaps it's not our group that Gaia needs," another woman told Hart. "There are hundreds of groups just like ours all across the country."

Hart was dumbfounded. Suddenly she remembered the voices she sometimes heard in the night as she searched the bands of her shortwave radio. Women's voices. Voices that talked about Sanctuary. Could it be possible that such a place really existed? "There are?" she asked, hardly daring to hope. "Where . . . how do you know this?"

"We know," Irena said decisively. "Oh yes, we know. Like always knows like. Am I too easy?"

Hart glared at the madwoman, then turned eagerly to Onava. "Is that right? Are there hundreds of groups? How do you contact each other?"

For an answer, Onava offered only an enigmatic smile. "We have our ways."

Exasperated, Hart shook her head. She couldn't imagine many groups could be left if they all shared Onava's beliefs. Surely some had a little more backbone, a greater love of freedom. "Do all these groups believe as you do?" she asked.

"We're all going to Sanctuary," Irena interjected. "To be with the angels. But the one with her hair on fire — oh beware. Red is not the Goddess's color. This angel will carry a sword and spill blood."

"Some believe as we do," Onava said. "Some are more . . . militant. And, yes, the BioStrike troopers have discovered many of us. It was inevitable. But some, we hope, are still hiding."

Hart was thunderstruck. So it was all true! Sometimes even she doubted the voices she heard — faint, filled with static, they could have been the voices of ghosts. It had taken Hart almost a year to figure out that all the voices were talking, cryptically, about the same thing — a place called Sanctuary. A place to which all the women were headed. Hart longed to contact these other women, but all her CQ messages — general calls to any station, the shortwave equivalent of yelling "Hello, out there!" were never acknowledged. Evidently these women knew a password of which she was ignorant, leaving her to listen in frustration. Excited, she made a mental note to come back to the subject of Sanctuary.

"How did the troopers find you?" Hart asked. "What happened?"

"Betrayal," Eda said bitterly. "There was a little community — not more than a hundred people — just down the mountain from the valley where we lived. We think someone sold us to the Californians. We did a lot of trading with the community," she explained. "We were their midwives, their healers. We trusted them."

"It couldn't have been in their best interests to betray you, then," Hart said, perplexed. "You helped each other."

Onava smiled sadly at Hart. "We never made any secret of the fact that we wanted to live apart from people. Nor did we make a secret of our pact with Gaia. Or of our love for each other."

"Your what?" Hart asked, puzzled.

"Our love for each other. Of course, we're lesbians."

Hart was silent. Of course, she thought. The townspeople would have been able to control their envy and rancor only so long. Watching their friends and family members die from the Red Death while the women on the mountain prospered would have been too much.

Hart recalled how the epidemic had started: at BioStrike, anyone exposed to the mist got the virus. Men, women, young, old — the organism respected no one. Thousands fell ill and died as the first wave of the Red Death hit. But in that initial wave of illness, Rafaela Harper, a physician in Los Angeles, observed

65

a curious phenomenon at her clinic. It was not mothers, or gay men, or ten-year-olds, or grandfathers who seemed to be the primary vector of this disease. Rather, it was young heterosexual males — the self-styled satyrs of the nineteen-nineties. Reprieved from the death sentence of AIDS by the HIV vaccine, young heterosexual men had seemingly spent most of the decade trying to make up for lost time. The number of cases of gonorrhea, syphilis, and herpes skyrocketed. But these were diseases which could be tolerated, they felt. After all, there *were* cures. Then, along came the Red Death. Despite Dr. Harper's warnings that the new disease was sexually transmitted, these young men didn't listen. Unlike gay men, they had never had to learn what "safe sex" meant, and it was through this group that the Red Death strode like a reaper through a field of wheat.

Hart remembered watching television rallies in which women marched carrying banners and signs that read "KEEP THE RED DEATH AWAY — SAY NO TO SEX!" Across the country, thousands of wives, mistresses, and girlfriends, terrified by the prospect that their men might be less than truthful about whom they had slept with last, said a resounding "No!" Women fled to nunneries, or formed "clean groups" and disappeared into the countryside, or locked the doors of their houses against their own husbands. Hart grimaced. The Red Death had brought about a new age of celibacy.

Hart looked around. Were Onava's women really lesbians? If so, it was likely that they would have remained free of the disease. Or were they heterosexual women — the remnants of the "clean

66

groups" who had fled the cities at the beginning of the epidemic? Hart found she wanted to ask questions, to know the facts. And did Onava's women, too, have their won Intimate Contact Regulations, similar to those that had been enacted at Tucson MedCenter? And if they didn't, how exactly had these women managed to stay free of the disease? Did they have no Stage Ones among them? How did they keep the Red Death out of their blood? She wanted to inquire, but was overcome by self-consciousness. Besides, she needed facts that might help her immediate situation more than she needed answers to these questions.

"How many women are here in this car?" Hart asked. "And are the other cars full, too?"

Onava looked at her and frowned, clearly disapproving of Hart's curiosity. "There are about twenty-five women here in this car," she said. "And fifteen or so in the car behind us. They're all from our group in Arizona. The car that holds your MedCenter team has only the three or four women medtechs in it. And Dr. Ashe. Then there's the car in which the men have been segregated — your driver, the male medtechs. The BioStrike Captain and her Lieutenant are in the command car, just behind the engine. And the last car is just an open flatbed — it has the BioStrike troopers' vehicles on it. The troopers sleep there too we're told."

Medina, Hart thought. Medina's here. She's safe. And Collins and the others. She came to a decision and stood up. Onava looked at her curiously as Hart walked to the door of the car.

"What do you intend to do?"

"Leave," Hart said, examining the door.

"It's not possible," Eda said, raising her voice and coming to join Hart. "They're always right there. You can't get away." She stood there, hands balled into fists. She wants to escape, Hart realized. She'd like to come with me. And she's angry with herself for having these feelings.

"We'll see," Hart told her. "I'm going to try." She looked around. Sensing something going on, most of the women in the car had turned to face Hart. Their faces glowed in the candlelight. Yet no one offered help. No one, apart from Eda, even spoke to her. Hart turned back to the door. It took her a moment to find the opening mechanism in the gloom, but when she saw it simply slid aside, she grasped the handle and pulled. Cool night air flooded into the car. The moon had just risen over the mountains, and by its cold silver light she saw the unmistakable shape of the station house. Onava was certainly right — they were still at the station. Crouching, Hart jumped from the car to the ground. "Well?" she said to the carload of women. "Arizona's just back there across the tracks. Anyone coming?"

No one answered. No one even moved. It was if the whole car were holding its breath.

"Eda?" Hart asked.

Moving to stand at the edge of the car, Eda looked longingly into the night. Then she closed her eyes and shook her head.

Hart turned away from her in disgust. On the other side of the tracks was Arizona. She had only to step between the cars and walk across the border. She looked both ways down the tracks. No BioStrike troopers were in sight.

She turned . . . and walked directly into the muzzle of a short-barreled rifle.

"Back in the car," the trooper told her.

Hart looked down at the muzzle of the rifle, then up at the impassive face of the trooper below the tipped-back visor. It was a thin, tight-lipped, pale face, black brows like smudges, frown lines between them. "No," Hart said. "I'm not going."

The trooper sighed heavily, and Hart thought she saw the woman's mouth turn down at the corners in a grimace. "Lau," she called out quietly.

Hart was grabbed forcefully from behind, one arm twisted up between her shoulder blades. "Don't do this," Hart said to the figure behind her. "You're making a mistake. I'm not one of those women on the train. I shouldn't be here. I'm an Arizonan."

"Get her in the car," the trooper with the rifle said to Lau. "Captain Sandoval wants to leave. There's a group of riders approaching from the east. As soon as our patrol gets back, we need to get underway." The trooper turned and left.

"Come on, now," Lau urged, not unkindly, forcing her back toward the car. "You heard Corporal Villanova. Just climb back in there. We've no time to waste."

At the open door of the car, Hart balked. "Help me!" she yelled out to the women inside. "There are only two of them out here. Rush them, for God's sake. They can't shoot all of you!"

Eda still stood in the doorway. Onava had come to join her, and the two women looked down at Hart with expressionless faces.

Lau made Hart step up to the open door of the

railroad car. The floor of the car came up to her chest, and looking up, Hart saw that Irena had come to join them. "Am I too easy, hair-on-fire?" she wailed to Hart, hugging herself and weeping.

In a flash of comprehension Hart saw that all the women had had a chance to escape when Lau and her fellow trooper had been busy with her. But not one of them had taken it! They're worse than cattle, Hart thought savagely. They deserve everything that's going to happen to them. The anger she had held back until now ignited in her like a flame.

"No!" she shouted. Letting her weight fall back against Lau, she drew her legs up to her chest, braced her feet against the side of the car, and pushed. Lau collapsed beneath her, crying out in pain, releasing her arm, and cursing. Rolling off Lau, Hart scuttled under the car and across the tracks. Breathing heavily, she crouched in the shadows, looking around frantically for cover. A clump of rocks and mesquite trees beckoned, maybe fifty feet away across a patch of open ground. Quickly, before she could change her mind, she scurried across, feeling naked and exposed. To her amazement no shots rang out, no voices demanded that she stop. Panting, she hid in the shadows. For the moment, anyhow, she was free.

CHAPTER 4

REPUBLIC OF CALIFORNIA
BIOSTRIKE EDICT NUMBER 106:
EUTHANASIA

All persons infected with the RD I virus are subject to euthanasia. BioStrike commanders are instructed to authorize their personnel to carry out this order with dispatch. The only exceptions are military personnel in Stage One of the disease. Such individuals are to be taken at once to an authorized Assessment and Treatment Center for transfusion.

71

* * * * *

Sandoval traded glares with the Tucson MedCenter physician — a wiry, weather-beaten, silver-haired woman named Ashe — and was childishly gratified when the other woman finally looked away. It's all in who blinks first, isn't it, she thought.

"I'm not going to cooperate," the Arizonan said in a tone of finality. "You're going to have to figure out how to do your own killing." Ashe crossed her arms over the front of her white coveralls, and looked at Sandoval in disgust.

"Madam," Sandoval said quietly, "I'm not asking you to cooperate. I'm telling you."

Ashe blinked again, and Sandoval saw the expression on the other woman's face alter, almost imperceptibly, to reflect uncertainty. So you're not as self-confident as you seem, Sandoval thought. Good. Ashe remained stonily silent.

"Private de la Rosa," Sandoval said, "take a trooper and go on back to the vehicles' flatbed. Go through the doctor's bag and the cabinets in the MedCenter vans, until you find what we need. And don't bother being neat about it."

"Yes, Ma'am," de la Rosa said, saluting crisply. "Private Barrios, come with me." Sandoval heard them hurry down the steps of the railway car.

"No," Ashe said to Sandoval. "You can't do this."

Sandoval raised an eyebrow. How predictable this all was. She felt a little ashamed of herself for bullying the doctor, but rationalized quickly that it couldn't be helped.

The doctor bowed her head. "Dammit, I can't

72

have those two brutes rifling my drug cabinet. I'll
give you what you want."

Sandoval motioned her out the door. "Lead the
way, Doctor."

Eyes front, Ashe preceded Sandoval out into the
gray dawn. As they walked down the tracks,
approaching the last car of the train where the
vehicles were secured, Sandoval smiled. Standing by
the door to the Tucson MedCenter van were de la
Rosa and Barrios.

"Dismissed," she told them. "Lieutenant Valentin
is in the engine car with Corporal Villanova. Tell
them I want steam up in an hour. And let Corporal
Lujan know that we're not chasing that solar tech."

"The solar tech?" Ashe asked, plainly startled.
"You don't mean Hart?"

"I believe that's her name," Sandoval said.

"She *escaped*?" Ashe sounded incredulous.

"Apparently," Sandoval replied acerbically. "She
seems most enterprising."

Ashe shook her head. In a moment she turned
back to Sandoval. "You tricked me," she accused.
"You never intended to rifle the drug cabinet."

Sandoval smiled ruefully. "I apologize, Doctor. But
it was necessary." She motioned Ashe onto the
flatbed.

With one final reproachful glance, Ashe climbed
onto the flatbed and wrenched open the door to one
of the MedCenter vans. Sandoval followed her inside.
The doctor opened one of the cabinets with a key on
a chain around her neck, and handed Sandoval a
small bottle and a syringe. "Cyanide," she said. "Do
try to hit the vein."

Sandoval put the bottle and the syringe in her breast pocket and closed the velcro flap.

"Listen," Ashe said, "are you sure about those men? Absolutely positive?"

Sandoval nodded. "Absolutely. We tested them twice. The results were the same — Red Death Positive, Stage One." She shrugged. "I can't afford to transfuse them. They're low priority. If it had been one of your medtechs . . ." She shrugged again. "Nonessential personnel infected with the Red Death are dispensable."

Ashe snorted. "Disposable is more like it."

Sandoval stared her down. "Call it what you please — including murder," she told the doctor. "I've heard it all before. You know as well as I do that those four men are a danger to us all. No one knows how far they've progressed into Stage One. That's all on their medical records back in Tucson. I'd love to be able to make use of their muscles — men *are* good for a few things — but I can't waste blood on them."

"So they're to be euthanized?"

"Yes."

Ashe looked at Sandoval in undisguised disgust. "How do you do it?"

"Do what? The euthanasia?"

"Hardly," Ashe said with a withering glance. "I mean this." She made a global gesture. "How do you carry out those despicable BioStrike Edicts we've heard so much about? How do you go on being a kidnapper and a butcher?"

Sandoval felt her lips twist in a smile. "It's my job, Doctor."

Ashe hooted. "Don't use that feeble excuse — it

74

won't wash. And besides, I didn't ask you why, I asked you how. You're clearly an intelligent woman — how can you do this? My God, I wonder how you can sleep at night with so many deaths on your conscience." She ran a hand through her hair.

Sandoval leaned back against the wall of the van, studying this little rooster of a woman. She was impressed — the doctor seemed absolutely unafraid. She liked people who weren't afraid of her. "All right, Doctor," she said, "I'll be more specific. I do this because I don't know another way of living with the Red Death. As abhorrent as these methods are, they've worked. We have a semblance of a government in California. We're struggling to reestablish the civilian population." She shrugged. "We all do what we have to. And I'm quite aware that that answer is simply an amplification of my previous answer. Another version of why. As for how, you'll have to forgive me if I give that a little thought. After all, you *are* a civilian. And you seem to believe we're on different sides."

Ashe looked at Sandoval quizzically. "Well, aren't we?"

"I have only one enemy, Doctor," Sandoval said. "The Red Death."

Ashe snorted. "And you'd do anything, sacrifice anyone, to defeat that enemy, would you?"

"As I said, I do what I have to do," Sandoval replied, acutely uncomfortable. Hell, she told herself — she thought as little of the Provisional Government's policies as did Dr. Ashe. Why was she being forced to justify them?

"This conversation goes round and round," Ashe said in vexation. "And I'm tired." She studied

Sandoval, a strange expression on her face. "I've just realized something — you hate it, don't you?" she said softly. "I see that now." She put her hands in her pockets and looked at Sandoval curiously.

Sandoval made a mask of her face and said nothing, wondering how she might have inadvertently betrayed her thoughts to this woman.

A bloodhound on a promising scent, Ashe continued. "If you hate it so much, let us go. Keep the bloody vaccine. It's obscene, what you're doing. Surely you know that."

Sandoval closed her eyes.

"Come with us back to Tucson," Ashe said. "Desert. Go AWOL. Bring your troopers. But for God's sake, Captain, let us go." She continued in a voice so quiet Sandoval had to strain to hear. "You must stop this, you know. It's destroying your soul."

Sandoval grimaced. "No. Even if I wanted to, I can't."

"Why not? What's preventing you?" Ashe wanted to know. "Some warped sense of duty?"

"I suppose you'd call it duty," Sandoval said, reaching behind her to open the door of the van. "Please, Doctor, it's time to go back." They walked together to the edge of the flatbed, Ashe preceding her.

"Honor," Ashe said, turning to face Sandoval, clearly wanting to understand. "If not duty, then honor. Am I right?"

"Perhaps," Sandoval equivocated. "That . . . and something else."

"Tell me," Ashe said. "I'd like this to make sense. You've taken my freedom from me — surely you owe me that much."

Sandoval looked into the woman's penetrating blue eyes. Yes, she did owe her that. "The BioStrike Force was created out of human detritus," she told Ashe. "Debris. Garbage. After the 'flu of ninety-nine, when there were so many homeless kids roaming the cities, and so much gang violence, some bright light got the idea that a youth corps to enforce the new health regulations would be effective. It would also get the kids off the streets. I was in the INS Border Patrol at the time of BioStrike, but was assigned to the new BioStrike Force as soon as it was created. My job — before I was sent to Sixth, on this border — was to comb the slums of California's cities, the prisons, the detention centers, looking for . . . suitable recruits." She laughed mirthlessly. "I found them. They enlisted willingly enough — after all, someone was offering to feed and clothe them, teach them some skills, and even *pay* them! And they soon learned what had happened to their friends who hadn't enlisted. They were simply never seen again. So those who had moral objections blinded themselves to this fact, and told themselves comfortable lies. It wasn't an army they were joining — it was something altogether new. A youth cadre — a force to change society." She laughed again. "Poor fools. If any of them had had the opportunity to read history, they might have elected to die in the slums or the prisons. The only difference between them — pardon me, us — and some of the other thugs of history is the color of our shirts." Self-conscious, aware that her explanation had become a lecture, she glared at Ashe. The doctor did not interrupt.

"Go on," Ashe urged.

Sandoval raised a skeptical eyebrow, but

continued. "At first we were to enforce the Surgeon General's 'Five Point Plan for Isolation of the Beijing Flu.' Nothing more." She shrugged. "Then BioStrike occurred, the world turned its back on us, and California closed its borders. We had new orders — enforce the BioStrike Edicts. So we did."

Sandoval took a deep breath. "But I digress. If I recall, you asked me what keeps me doing this job. You wondered if it was honor. I wonder about that, too. Do you know, Doctor, that my aide, Corporal Lujan, is only nineteen? Sixteen of my privates are twenty or younger. My other corporal is twenty-one. As grotesque as you may find this fact, the BioStrike Force has been the only positive thing in their lives. Before they joined up, they lived on the streets, or behind bars. They were whores, pickpockets, thieves, drug dealers, murderers. I personally recruited these women. I picked them for the Sixth. I told them that things would be better if they came with me." Sandoval stopped speaking, aware that she had said far too much.

She hadn't meant to tell the doctor all this, and was angry with herself for having done so. And she hadn't told Ashe the worst part — that the BioStrike units were now used for the dirtiest, riskiest jobs: euthanasia of Stage Ones, "patriation" of other states' RD negatives, incarceration of California's pure-blood citizens. And then there were the donor camps, or in BioStrike Edict parlance, the Assessment and Treatment Facilities — facilities meant only for military and Provisional Government personnel. The reluctant donors were kept there under armed BioStrike guard and the responsibility for maintaining order in the camps rested entirely with the BioStrike

78

Forces. Sandoval shuddered. Things could be worse, she supposed — she could be commander of the Los Angeles A & 'T facility.

Ashe's brows were knit in a frown. "I had no idea . . ." she said quietly.

Sandoval decided abruptly to go on, to tell the doctor more. What difference could it possibly make? "In the beginning, the BioStrike Forces actually seemed to do some good. We kept order. We kept things going. But now . . .' Sandoval grimaced. "There's no one left who believes we're doing the right thing anymore." She gestured back at the train. "Not even the very young ones, like Lujan."

Ashe looked at Sandoval in evident horror. "Then why do Lujan and the others carry on?"

Sandoval laughed aloud this time, a short, sharp bark. "Because Captain Zia Sandoval recruited them. Because Captain Zia Sandoval gives them their orders. Does that surprise you? To learn that they do what they do because they're loyal to me? I have nothing to offer them but a glorious apocalypse — a short military career, and a bloody end. And still they're loyal." She shook her head. "That should have been your question — it's so much more appropriate. You should have asked me how *I* can do this: how *I* can order them to kidnap and murder and incarcerate innocent civilians. After all, I'm the one ultimately responsible. Well, Doctor? Any guesses?"

Ashe shook her head, clearly sobered by Sandoval's vehemence.

Grimly, Sandoval continued. "No? No moralizing about honor? No more wondering about how I sleep at night, or how I can bear to look in the mirror?"

"No," Ashe said, avoiding Sandoval's eyes.

It was Sandoval's turn to be disgusted. "Go on back to your moralistic fellow Arizonans — the remnants of your perfect conservative society. You, I imagine, have no trouble sleeping at night. At least your conscience is clear."

She turned from Ashe and looked up the tracks. "Private Lau!" she shouted. A young trooper with straight black hair and almond-shaped dark eyes came hurrying along the tracks. "Take the doctor back to the Arizonans." She favored Lau with a frown. "And try not to lose this one."

"Yes, Captain," Lau said, saluting and hurrying away with Ashe.

Sandoval walked slowly back to the command car, thinking over what Ashe had said. Honor? Hardly. Loyalty? Certainly not to the Provisional Government in Los Angeles. What, then? She sighed. Because she had to do *something*. As repugnant as her duties were, they constituted a struggle. A fight against an awesome foe. But, she acknowledged, after three years of struggle, God knows she was sick to death of the fight.

* * * * *

Sandoval looked at the four men huddled in an uncertain group under a mesquite tree. Three wore the white coveralls of the medtech crew, and one, an older man, the same sort of gray coveralls the solar tech had worn.

"The BioStrike Edicts compel me to euthanize you," she told them. "You are all Stage One Positive."

One of the young medtechs, a burly blond, began

to cry. She looked at him briefly in disgust, then addressed herself to the tech in gray.

"I have no stomach for this sort of killing," she said. "What's your name?"

"Collins, Ma'am," the tech answered.

"Here," she said, handing him a pistol. He took it in amazement. "About a hundred yards down the trail from here, you'll find four survival packs. We took them from your vans."

"I see," Collins said in surprise. "So you're giving us a fighting chance."

"Yes," she said decisively. Even though it was treason. She snorted. Treason. The word held little meaning for her any more. Right, wrong — those were the important concepts. "Go on down the trail and find those survival packs," she told them. "Wait for Collins there." After the men had gone, she turned back to Collins. "Here," she said, handing him a handful of shells for the pistol. "Put these in your pocket."

Collins weighed them in his hand. "Aren't you afraid I'll load the gun and shoot you?" he asked.

"No," she told him. "I'm not afraid of that."

Smiling sheepishly, he put the shells in a pocket.

She stepped behind the tree, found the packet Lujan had hidden there, and handed it to Collins. "The map is marked with the locations of all known outlaw camps," she said. "Stay clear of them. But once you get away from the border you should have no trouble." She reached into her breast pocket and removed the syringe and bottle of clear fluid which Ashe had given her. "Put this someplace safe," she told him. "I'm assuming one of the medtechs will know how to administer this." She looked at Collins meaningfully. "If it becomes necessary, you can perform your own euthanasia."

He took the bottle and the syringe and put them carefully in a pocket. "Thank you," he said. "You didn't have to do this."

She gave him a crooked smile. "I'm not certain you'll thank me in a few days, after your water runs low. But good luck to you anyway."

* * * * *

"Captain Sandoval!" a young trooper called urgently, running up the tracks, almost falling into Sandoval's arms. Her black uniform was covered with a film of ochre dust, and the goggles she had worn had left a white mask in the brown dirt of her face. One skinned cheek was caked with dried blood. "Private Estefan, reporting, Ma'am." Panting, she saluted crisply.

"Report, Private Estefan," Sandoval urged, her pulse accelerating.

"It's the patrol, Ma'am. Corporal Rincon and the others. They've been pinned down by a force of mounted civilians about a mile south of here. In the arroyo."

Sandoval hoped her voice betrayed none of her apprehension. "Casualties?"

Estefan shook her head. "None yet, Ma'am. The civilians seem afraid to get too close. They're sniping from a distance. They have my night glasses," she added. "And Wilkins's too. They took us both prisoner, but I escaped." Only a twitch under her eye betrayed her anger. "The patrol is pretty well pinned down."

"How many?" Sandoval asked.

"Sixteen men and horses," Estefan answered promptly.

"And the patrol?"

"Corporal Rincon, and Privates Johnson, Garces, Mendoza, and Hawley. And three overland vehicles."

Sandoval massaged her temples. "Thank you, Estefan. Go and have some food and water now. And see that you get your face taken care of."

Estefan touched her cheek. "Oh. Yes, Ma'am. I'd forgotten about that." She hesitated for a moment, clearly diffident. "Ma'am?"

"Yes, Estefan?"

"May I — that is, I'd like to formally request to be included in the rescue party."

"Rescue party?" Sandoval asked, her thoughts racing in three directions at once. "Did I say anything about a rescue party?"

"No, Ma'am. But everyone knows you'd never abandon one of your troopers. And I feel responsible for Wilkins. If it hadn't been for me, she wouldn't have been taken prisoner. So I thought . . ."

Sandoval gave the young trooper a stern look. "You're dismissed, Estefan."

Estefan's face fell, and an expression of uncertainty came into her eyes. Her shoulders slumped, then she recovered her composure, and stood up straight. She saluted, turning smartly on her heel to go.

Sandoval let her take three steps before she spoke. "As soon as you're able, go to the command car and see Corporal Lujan," Sandoval told Estefan's retreating back. "I want a sketch of that arroyo — I want to know about the terrain. Everything you remember."

Estefan turned and gave her a dazzling smile. "Yes, *Ma'am*."

Sandoval rubbed her temples again. God. All she wanted was to sleep. She'd been up all night with the Tucson MedCenter contingent, arguing with that intractable Ashe woman. And supervising the blood harvesting. She tried to suppress the stab of guilt she felt at using one of the state's newly acquired possessions — the Arizonan donor Hart — for her own purposes. But in Sandoval's mind, it was all the same. What her troopers needed, she needed.

Lujan and three of the others had a blood reading of RD positive, Stage One. Even though the virus was largely inactive, it was still in their bloodstreams. Monthly transfusions from RD negative donors might keep things in more or less a state of equilibrium. For a time. But how long would it be before the new symptoms appeared? The virus might die, but — and Sandoval dreaded the much more common outcome — suddenly become active. She couldn't stomach the thought of Lujan and the others becoming Stage Twos, bearing on their bodies the first outward signs of the Red Death — bloody blisters that would appear almost overnight, signaling the beginning of the end. If that happened, the disease was extremely contagious, and could easily be transmitted by touch. Paradoxically, that phase of Stage Two would disappear after thirty-six hours, the blisters heal, and normal health seemingly be restored. But it would be false health. All it would mean was that the disease was at work within, destroying vital organs. And then, the only unknown would be which organ, or

84

major system, would give way first. The record for survival beyond this stage of the disease was, as Sandoval recalled, three days. The only good thing that could be said about the Red Death was that it was a quick killer.

Sandoval remembered that in the early months after BioStrike, Red Death victims often assumed, erroneously, that they had somehow shaken off the disease when its first outward signs vanished. And cruelest of all, they felt well. They had no idea that their bodies were riddled with sickness, and that they were being eaten from within. Only when their kidneys or lungs or hearts succumbed to the disease did they realize, in shock and terrible pain as some major body system failed, that they had been duped. Because of the telltale red blisters of Stage Two, and because the sufferers' deaths were always bloody — blood coughed up or excreted — the disease had become known as the Red Death.

Sandoval shuddered. Lujan's fine young face covered with bloody marks? She shook her head. Not if she could help it. No, in the absence of an A & T facility, she had done what she had to do — she used one of the new donors for harvesting. The actual transfusion wasn't due for a few days yet. What the hell, she shrugged. She'd put it in her report. Let BioStrike Central make what they wanted of it.

* * * * *

Sandoval crouched in the shadow of a palo verde and raised her binoculars. In the arroyo, about two hundred yards away, barricaded by a clump of boulders and the OLVs, was Sandoval's patrol. A pair

85

of civilian riflemen, dressed in khaki uniforms, each
with a large black cross on the back of his shirt,
sniped at the troopers from behind a fallen tree on
the arroyo's bank. Sandoval recognized them —
members of the Purification Church. Their leader, a
mad misogynist named Taber, had declared — despite
a mountain of evidence to the contrary — that
women were the source of the Red Death contagion.
This particular philosophy had attracted a greater
following than Sandoval would have believed, and in
the early days following BioStrike, the PC's ranks
swelled. Now the Red Death had taken its toll on
even the devout followers of the Purification Church
— thereby disproving Taber's theory — but several
PC groups were still active on the border, bringing
purification — and death — to female BioStrike
troopers and donors alike. Sandoval had tangled four
or five times with these madmen.

"Where are the other civilians?" Sandoval asked.

"Over there," Estefan whispered. "On the right
bank of the arroyo. In that clump of saguaro."

"I see them," Sandoval said.

A bloodcurdling scream pierced the air — a
woman's scream, full of agony and despair.

Sandoval ground her teeth in frustration. To her
immense satisfaction, not one of her troopers spoke.
Not one of them asked "Who's that?" or "What are
they doing to her?" They knew. It was one of their
fellow troopers. Every one of them was familiar with
the PC's practices — they knew very well what was
being done.

Valentin materialized beside her, panting a little,
surprising Sandoval. Fine drops of sweat beaded
Valentin's upper lip and her light blue eyes sparkled

with excitement. She loves this, Sandoval thought in dismay. Dammit. I should have ordered her to stay at the train supervising engine repairs. She shook her head. Valentin seemed to have her own agenda — prepared no doubt by BioStrike Central. Sandoval judged it best to let her pursue it.

"Report," Sandoval told the private accompanying Valentin.

"Yes, Captain. More than half the camp is still asleep. As far as I can make out, only the two snipers, and the three men with . . . with our trooper are awake."

"We could take them now," Valentin said eagerly. "Fall on them while they're asleep. Wipe them all out."

"Oh, we could, could we?" Sandoval queried. "Private Jing — see if you can raise our patrol on the radio. Go on back down the trail where the sound is less likely to carry. Tell Corporal Rincon that we're going to pick off the two snipers who are pinning them down. Tell them to be ready to move out as soon as they hear three shots." Jing saluted, picked up the radio, and hurried back down the trail.

"Private Flores — take our best two shooters. Get behind those snipers and silence them." She looked at her watch — as much to check the time as to avoid having to look at Valentin. "Give us fifteen minutes, Flores. After you signal the patrol, get back to your OLVs and get out of here. Don't wait for us. We'll be along."

Flores saluted. "Yes, Ma'am," she said, hurrying away.

"And me?" Valentin inquired. "Have you no orders for me?"

Sandoval looked briefly at Valentin, then raised her binoculars again. "Yes, Lieutenant Valentin. I have orders for you. You are to proceed back to the OLVs and wait for us. Under no circumstances are you to become involved in this action. You may observe, but that's all."

Valentin said nothing.

Sandoval lowered her binoculars and turned to look at Valentin. "Did I make myself clear, Lieutenant?"

Valentin blinked, an unreadable emotion surfacing briefly behind her eyes. "Yes, Captain," she replied, smiling a small secretive smile.

"Come on, Private Estefan," Sandoval said. "Let's leave these troopers to their work."

* * * * *

"Six minutes until Flores knocks off those snipers," Estefan said, turning her head to whisper in Sandoval's ear.

"I know," Sandoval said, peering through the bushes. The three civilians had taken Wilkins about a hundred yards away from the main camp, into the shelter of a large clump of boulders, no doubt to purify her in privacy. Wilkins, minus shirt, boots, and weapons, lay face up and unmoving on the ground. Sandoval grunted. She could see that her lip was split. It had bled freely, and the lower part of her face looked ghoulish. One eyebrow was bloody, and a large discolored bruise had formed on the young trooper's temple. Not a good sign. The three men lounged on the ground, laughing and chatting.

88

"Take off your jacket and shirt," she told Estefan. "And your weapons belt. Leave everything here."

Estefan obeyed, only her eyes asking questions. She dropped everything at Sandoval's feet. Sandoval had a brief impression of high young breasts before she put the binoculars to her eyes again. "Take your pistol and stuff it down the back of your pants," she told Estefan. "Now, just start walking toward the men. Hold your hands in the air. And jiggle your breasts a little."

Estefan clearly understood. She grinned at Sandoval and shoved her pistol into the waistband of her pants.

"At fifty feet, shoot the one with the tattoo on his chest," Sandoval told Estefan. "Then go get Wilkins. Take her to the rendezvous point. I'll take care of those other two PC heroes and join you. Ready?"

"Yes, Ma'am," Estefan said.

Sandoval smiled at her, and briefly gripped her bare shoulder. "Go on then, trooper. And don't cross my line of fire."

Estefan stood up from the cover of the bushes and started walking, making no effort to be silent or inconspicuous. At fifty yards, the man with the tattoo saw her.

"Jesus Christ!" he said, rolling to his knees. "Look at that."

Sandoval smiled, bringing her rifle up to her cheek and sighting.

At thirty yards, Estefan waved at the men. "Hey," she called. "I got something for you."

Sandoval groaned. No theatrics, damn it, she said

under her breath, positioning the rifle butt against her shoulder. She centered the cross-hairs of the scope on the second man, the blond, and steadied her breathing.

"Come on, baby," the blond said, rising to his feet. "Let's see what else you got." All three men were standing now, gaping at Estefan, grinning hugely. Like targets on a rifle range, Sandoval thought.

The third man, the youngest, put his hands on his hips and laughed. "Shit," he said, "don't she have any friends?"

Sandoval counted. Fifty-five . . . fifty . . . shoot, damn it, Estefan. But the young woman kept walking forward. Sandoval cursed.

Then several things happened at once. Two shots rang out from the direction of the arroyo, then three shots together.

"Keeping them busy, I guess," the man with the tattoo commented.

Sandoval saw Estefan reach behind her, grab the butt of her pistol and bring it around to aim at the tattooed man. It *boomed* once, and Sandoval saw the muscles in Estefan's back stand out as she fought the big gun's recoil.

Smoothly, Sandoval squeezed the trigger. Through the scope she saw the blond man fall, a red flower blossoming on his chest. The last one, the young one, had a chance. He could have run for cover. But he fell to his knees, scrambling frantically over to the pile of discarded shirts, belts, and weapons, choosing fight over cover. Sandoval shot him in the back as he tried to pull a pistol from its holster. Taking one last

90

look through the scope she saw Estefan half-carrying
Wilkins off into the brush. Rising to her feet, she
scooped up the young trooper's belongings, and
hurried after her.

CHAPTER 5

Savage are they who save only themselves.
Leonardo da Vinci, *The Notebooks*

Thirsty, hot, tired, and anxious, Hart crouched among the boulders, wondering what to do. She had spent the better part of the morning dozing fitfully in the shade, head resting on her arms, starting every time she heard a noise from the California side of the tracks. But so far, apart from a party of troopers who had departed on bulky, noisy land-crawlers, and the occasional hiss of steam from the engine car, nothing had happened. What were they doing, she wondered. What were they waiting for?

For that matter, what was *she* waiting for? Now that she was free, why wasn't she on her way back to Tucson? She slapped at an insect buzzing around her nose. The prospect of walking five hundred miles through the desert was unattractive under the best of circumstances. And these circumstances were about the worst Hart could imagine: she had no food, no water, no compass, no matches, no weapons. Some of the things she was lacking could be improvised: food could always be found along the way; a weapon of sorts could be fabricated; a fire could be made. The limiting factor, however, was water. From her desert survival classes at Tucson MedCenter, she was confident that she could survive a trek of that length. But not without water.

And there was another complication. She knew that bands of outlaws had erected makeshift settlements along the border. They detained hapless RD negatives there, and sold their blood to the highest bidder — often the BioStrike Forces. She had no idea where these camps were. It would be just her luck to stumble into one of them.

But the biggest obstacle to her departure was her reluctance to leave behind the known for the unknown. Even though the known in this case was little better than a prison sentence. Life as a blood donor, in some filthy California camp? She shuddered. Surely flight, even flight to nowhere, was preferable to a life lived like that. But flight meant leaving Dr. Ashe and Medina behind. She knew very well that she would probably never see either of them again.

She looked over the tops of the boulders at the

train and for one instant she was tempted to surrender. They had food and water there, a defeatist voice whispered to her. And she had escaped once — couldn't she do it again? Stop it, she told the voice roughly. I won't even consider giving myself up. There has to be another way. But what?

From her vantage point in the boulders, she could see the MedCenter vans, and her service van, too, secured on the flatbed. If the MedCenter vans were anything like hers and Collins's, there was plenty of food and water in them. After all, the MedCenter personnel had to eat and drink on the way back. Her heart began to beat faster. Yes — that was the answer. She'd worm her way over to the vans, rifle the food supplies for something portable, appropriate the survival kit. It contained, as she recalled, a knife, a compass, a map, matches, snakebite anti-venom, and first aid supplies. Then she'd get her jacket, as much water as she could carry, and the pistol Collins always kept under the driver's seat. Suddenly the walk back to Tucson didn't seem so insurmountable. As for the outlaw camps, she'd just have to be careful.

Raising her head slowly above the boulders, she looked around. No one seemed to be paying any attention to this side of the train. She circled around behind the rocks, took another cautious look, then, satisfied the way was clear, sprinted for the flatbed. Scrambling up onto the dusty platform, she rolled underneath one of the vans and lay there on her stomach, panting. Looking around, she noted with relief that there were no booted BioStrike trooper feet in evidence. The flatbed was clearly unguarded. Good, she thought, squirming out from under the van.

Standing up, she found the van marked SERVICE, and cautiously tried the back door. Locked. Creeping around the side of the vehicle, she tried the passenger side door. Also locked. Damn. She retraced her path around the back of the van, then tried the driver's door. It opened. Gratefully, she climbed inside, then crawled between the seats to the back.

The supplies she and Collins had packed for the trip were just where they'd left them — in a cupboard in the back of the van. Suppressing guilty thoughts of Collins, she unscrewed the top of one of the water bottles and held it to her mouth. She couldn't swallow fast enough, and some of the water ran out over her lips and trickled down the neck of her coveralls. She drank until the bottle was empty. Eyes tearing, she set the bottle down, wiped her mouth, and opened the supplies cupboard. Selecting a dehydrated apple and grain cereal, she added a little water to it from a new bottle, then forced herself to wait. When at last it was soft enough to eat, she wolfed it down with her fingers, then tore open a packet of dehydrated chicken stew, added water, and ate it, too. The saltiness of the stew tasted good, and Hart prepared another, eating this one more slowly while she took stock.

There was a variety of dehydrated meal packets remaining: three apple and grain cereal, six chicken stew, four assorted beans, four cheese, two mixed berries, and four chopped nuts. Also, there was some cornmeal and a little salt. Hart put all the food into a carryall bag, added the survival kit, and was just preparing to load the water bottles when she heard the sounds of engines in the distance, racing up the arroyo. She raised her head above the level of the back window. Damn! The troopers were returning on their overland vehicles. Frantically she tidied the mess she had created with the food packets, made a dive into the front of the van for Collins's gun, checked the load, and stuffed the weapon into a pocket of her coveralls. Then she heaved her bag of supplies onto one of the overhead bunks where it wouldn't be noticed wedged against the ceiling, and rolled under the rear seat, making herself as small as she could.

The troopers drove the OLVs up to the edge of the flatbed and someone put a ramp in place. Hart felt the flatbed shake as the vehicles were driven onto the train. Finally all the engines were shut off. Hart heard the sounds of the troopers talking quietly among themselves.

"She's bleeding pretty badly, Ma'am," a voice said. "Maybe we shouldn't move her any more."

"Very well, Flores," a crisp, authoritative voice said. Hart froze. She recognized that voice — it was the voice of the BioStrike commander, the one whom Hart had spoken to just before she was shot. "Lieutenant Valentin, go on up to the engine car and tell Villanova to get up steam and move us out of here. Immediately. And on your way, send someone for that Arizona physician and a couple of assistants. We're going to use one of these MedCenter vans as an operating room. Flores, see that the brakes are set on all these vehicles, and put blocks under the wheels. And get the power on in these two vans. We'll use one as an OR and one as a recovery room."

Hart heard the sounds of van doors being opened and closed, and tried her best to breathe quietly. Someone entered her van by the driver's door, set the brake, and left. All of a sudden sounds of cursing erupted outside.

"What do you mean there's no power?" the BioStrike commander yelled. "The sun's shining, isn't it? Doesn't this unit make power from sunshine?"

"Yes, Ma'am, but no one understands how to work it. That Arizona solar tech did, but she's escaped," an apologetic voice replied. "And, well, we can't understand the manuals. They're too technical."

"Damn it all to bloody hell!" the commander erupted. "Well, Ashe will just have to work without power."

"Impossible, I'm afraid, Captain," a new voice said. Dr. Ashe's voice. "I need power for the lights, for the air filters, to sterilize my instruments, to keep the van cool. Medina, go inside and take a temperature reading." Hart's spirits lifted. It was good to hear that Ashe and Medina were all right.

"It's almost one hundred and ten in here," Medina called out.

"Impossible, Captain," Ashe repeated.

"Stop telling me what you can't do," the commander told her in a voice so full of menace that Hart shivered. "I have two troopers here with bullet wounds, and another who needs to be assessed for possible concussion. Medical procedures certainly took place before the era of electric lights and air conditioning."

"I think I'm a little more familiar than you with the subject of emergency medicine," Ashe said testily.

"Listen to me, Doctor," the commander said. "You have ten seconds to make up your mind. If you won't treat these troopers, Flores and I will. She's had a little training in battlefield medicine, and I have a strong stomach and a steady hand. We'd prefer to have your expertise, but we can get along without it. Well?"

Hart held her breath. Would Ashe and Medina cooperate with this fearsome woman? Or would they turn their backs on the troopers? She was willing to bet which choice the intractable Medina would make. But what about Ashe?

"Once again, you win, Captain," Ashe said in a bitter voice.

"No, Doctor, they win," the Captain replied. "Tell me what you require."

"I need that bloody solar tech, as you so unkindly described her. The one you so foolishly let escape," Ashe said. "She's the only one who knows how to operate these units. Hell — she designed them! We have to get them working."

Hart closed her eyes. No! She wouldn't be tempted. She intended to use the first opportunity that presented itself for escape. After all, wasn't it every prisoner's duty to escape? If there were only some way that she could creep outside, reset the collector switches on the tops of the MedCenter vans, creep back inside, collect her bag, and be gone. But there wasn't. In a few moments there would be so much activity around the vans that she would be spotted for sure. There was no time to be generous.

She rolled out from under the seat, collected her bag from the top of the bunk, filled the water bottles, and stuffed her jacket into the bag, zipping it shut. She put her arms through the straps, and settled it against her back, grunting a little at the weight. Well, it couldn't be helped. As soon as she started to drink the water, she reflected wryly, her load would lighten considerably. She took a quick look outside. No one was in sight. Probably they were still making preparations. Quietly opening the back door of the van she stepped outside, closing it after her. The ground was tantalizingly close — she had only to jump to the hard-packed earth, sprint to the first bush, then weave her way back to the pile of boulders. But she hesitated. How long could it take to reset the collector switches? I'll just take a look, she told herself. If anyone's there, I'll forget about it.

Peering around the corner of her van, she wasn't sure if she was disappointed or relieved when she saw no one. Sighing, she slipped off her pack and lowered it to the floor of the flatbed. If Medina could only see me now, she thought ruefully. As quietly as she could, she crept up to the back of the first MedCenter van, climbed the ladder, and wriggled under the solar collectors. The reset switch was in a box on top of the van, near the base of one of the collectors, and she opened the box, noting that the COLLECTOR ON light was glowing red. Good. She pressed the button marked RESET, then the switch marked BATTERY BYPASS, and last, the button marked POWER ON. A reassuring hum came from the ceiling beneath her, and she wriggled back out from under the collector and climbed down the ladder. Trying the door of the MedCenter van, she found it unlocked. She hesitated. Hurry, she told herself. Finish it. Turning the power on is no good at all if you don't turn on the interior equipment. She closed the door softly, and crossed to the wall panel. Making certain the storage batteries were being bypassed, she turned everything on: lights, cooling unit, blood storage unit, medical equipment. There, she told herself. It'll run till doomsday. One down, one to go.

She was starting to climb the ladder to the second MedCenter van, when the train whistled urgently three times, and gave a lurch that almost threw her from the ladder. Damn — the train was getting ready to pull out. Hart flew through the steps she had performed with the first van, and was at the second van's interior equipment panel when the door was wrenched open behind her back.

"And just who the hell are you?"

Hart looked back over her shoulder. Dr. Ashe. She straightened up and smiled. "Hello."

"Hart!" Ashe exclaimed. "They told us you'd escaped. What in hell are you doing back here?"

Hart gestured at the interior of the van. "Turning the equipment on. The power and the cooling units."

"Jesus Christ," Ashe exclaimed. "That took guts. That martinet Sandoval will be back here any minute." She ran a hand through her hair. "Hart, what are we going to do with you? Maybe we can hide you somewhere."

Hart frowned. "What do you mean? I'm going back to MedCenter. I'll get help. I'll tell them . . ." She trailed off, suddenly remembering. She felt as though the bottom had fallen out of her stomach.

"What's wrong?" Ashe asked, gripping her arm.

"MedCenter," Hart whispered. "I can't go back there and ask for help. They know all about this. Those men in the unmarked van." She licked her lips, feeling sick. "Dr. Ashe, they set this up!"

Ashe gaped at Hart. "What are you talking about?"

Hart looked away, ashamed. "I . . . overheard

100

them talking. I was on top of another van, fixing the panels."

"Hart!" Ashe whispered in dismay. "Why didn't you tell us?"

Miserable, Hart closed her eyes for a moment. "I couldn't," she said lamely. "I had a chance, but I couldn't." Opening her eyes, she looked at Ashe. "I was afraid."

Ashe took her in her arms and hugged her tight. "Oh, Hart," she said.

"I'm sorry," Hart told her, clamping her eyes shut on the tears.

Ashe patted Hart on the back, then gripped her shoulders, stepping away. "Never mind," she said, her face grim. "What's done is done. Now, the best thing you could do for yourself is to run. But if what you say is true, you certainly can't go back to MedCenter."

"Where, then?" Hart asked, feeling desperate.

Ashe gave Hart a level look, and Hart felt that for the first time Ashe saw her as something other than a child. "Yuma," Ashe said. "Southwest Health Facility. Ask for Dr. Yolanda Castillo. You'll probably make it." Ashe smiled sadly. "But you'd better go if you're going."

Hart hesitated. Yuma — another contingent of strangers. But Ashe was right. She needed to leave now, while she still could. As if to underscore the urgency of the situation, the train gave another disconcerting lurch.

The van door opened behind Ashe, and Hart expected to see Captain Sandoval stride through it. But it was Medina.

"Hart," Medina exclaimed in evident relief. "They told us you'd gotten away."

"I had," Hart said.

"She only came back to reset the collectors," Ashe told Medina. "With any luck she'll be safe in Yuma in a couple of days. So say goodbye. I'm about to boot her off this train."

"Hart!" Medina said, plainly appalled. "You can't go. We need you. No one else knows how to run this equipment."

The train lurched again, then settled into a slow, steady rhythm. Hart looked frantically out the van window at the desert passing by.

"Hart, please," Medina asked.

"You didn't tell me this," Hart accused Ashe. "Is it true?"

Ashe shrugged. "We could get along without you. But if you stayed, of course things would be easier."

"But . . . Captain Sandoval . . ." Hart said fearfully. She clenched her fists. Why should she be the one to make such difficult decisions? This just wasn't fair. If she stayed, she'd risk being caught all over again. How long could she hope to avoid detection by Sandoval? And what would the BioStrike Captain do to her once she was discovered? Throw her back with the Gaians? But the thought of Yuma, of people she didn't know, of a facility in which she had no place, daunted her. She took one last look at Medina's tense, worried face and thought of what she owed Dr. Ashe. "All right!" she shouted. Then, after a moment, she answered more calmly, "All right. I'll stay."

PART TWO
THE JOURNEY

CHAPTER 6

One cannot be too careful in one's choice of enemies.
Oscar Wilde,
The Picture of Dorian Gray

Sandoval paced the length of the command car, looking out the window now and then. The tracks climbed up the side of a ravine. On one side was sheer rock — so near Sandoval could have reached out and touched it. On the other was a ravine whose hillside was dotted with pines and oaks. She shuddered. She never had liked heights. But at least they were in motion — that was the good news. The bad news was that Villanova had reported that the engine repairs would not hold. She had done what she could, she said, but without parts, the likelihood was that this train would never reach Los Angeles. Sandoval swore, checking herself as her pacing carried her to the partition that divided her part of the car from Valentin's.

Just then, the young lieutenant appeared from around a corner of the partition and leaned against it, watching Sandoval impassively. "A problem?" she inquired.

Sandoval considered keeping quiet about the engine trouble, but saw no reason to deceive Valentin. Besides, she would know about it soon enough. "The engine," she said. "It won't get us back to L.A."

"Oh?" Valentin replied, raising one blonde eyebrow. "I thought Villanova had it fixed."

"She thought so, too," Sandoval said flatly. "But she claims a part suddenly disappeared."

Valentin laughed. "Disappeared? She misplaced it, more likely."

Sandoval shook her head. "Villanova's never been known to misplace anything."

Valentin shrugged. "What then — sabotage?"

Sandoval looked at Valentin in surprise. Until now she had never thought of sabotage. Who would want to tamper with the engine? It would be suicide. They would be stranded in the middle of the desert, hundreds of miles from any BioStrike outpost. And in this case, they would be at the mercy of the very civilians they sought to escape. The idea was ludicrous. Or was it? Sandoval shrugged. "I hadn't considered it," she told Valentin.

"It seems unlikely," Valentin answered. "But it's best to consider all possibilities, don't you agree?"

"Mmmm," Sandoval said thoughtfully.

"So what happens after the engine gives out?" Valentin inquired, flicking an invisible piece of lint off one shirt sleeve.

Sandoval laughed. "Then we walk." She moved to stand in front of a map pinned to the wall of the car. "Although, I might add, there's very little to walk to."

Valentin came to join her. "Indio," she suggested. "There's a BioStrike unit there. Or Palm Springs. That's Southwest A & T headquarters."

"When was the last time you were down I-10?" Sandoval asked.

"I've never been down I-10," Valentin replied, an amused tone in her voice. "What does that have to do with anything?"

"Everything — the road's impassible after Desert Center."

"Oh?" Valentin answered. "Even to the OLVs?"

Sandoval turned to look at Valentin, frankly puzzled. "Lieutenant, we have a couple dozen civilians with us. What do you suggest we do with them while the rest of us go ahead on the OLVs?"

Valentin shrugged, eyes on the map. "I'm suggesting nothing. I was merely asking for information."

Not bloody likely, Sandoval thought. What game are you playing, Valentin?

"What about the Salton Sea?" Valentin asked, pointing. "There was an old naval base there. Now it's a Donor Holding Facility."

Sandoval sighed. "Valentin, be reasonable. We're

going to have to march the civilians overland in the heat. That is, if we make it through the mountain pass. As I see it, we have only two or three choices." She looked at Valentin, examining her with interest. What kind of creature are you, she wondered. The young lieutenant looked from the map to Sandoval, pale blue eyes expressionless. Sandoval came to a decision. "I think I'm going to leave you in charge of this problem, Lieutenant," Sandoval said. "I have to go down to our field hospital. Have some suggestions for me when I return."

Valentin nodded. "Yes, Captain." She turned back to study the map. "Captain Sandoval," she called just as Sandoval was preparing to leave.

"Yes, Lieutenant?" Sandoval said wearily. With Valentin there was always something else.

Valentin took two steps forward, stopped, and put her hands in her pockets. She looked directly at Sandoval, making no attempt to conceal her dislike. "Why did you refuse to let me be a part of the operation in the arroyo? And why did you reject my suggestion?"

Sandoval raised an eyebrow. "I've read your dossier, Lieutenant. I know why BioStrike Central sent you here. At least I know what your orders say. But that's military double-talk. For what it's worth, Valentin, I believe I know the true reason you were sent here." Might as well give her something to think about, Sandoval thought wryly.

"Do you indeed?" Valentin asked quietly, a superior smile playing about her lips.

Sandoval came close to losing her temper then. Just be calm, she told herself. "Lieutenant, I know what your official orders state. You are to observe the

108

Sixth BioStrike Unit in action, and report back to BioStrike Central. I'm certain you have unofficial orders. My earlier statement notwithstanding, those orders are no concern of mine. What is a concern of mine is the welfare of my troopers. Allowing you — a junior officer with no field experience — to take part in the operation in the arroyo would have been foolhardy. I selected only troopers who had been seasoned in firefights. How many firefights have you been in, Lieutenant?" She waited, aware that she was making Valentin lose face. To hell with it, she thought savagely. You asked for this confrontation, not me.

"None," Valentin answered through clenched teeth. "But you know that."

"Precisely," Sandoval replied. "And as for rejecting your suggestion, I did so for the same reason. Your lack of experience."

"I see," Valentin said, making no effort to disguise her sarcasm. "Thank you for making things clear."

"You're welcome, Lieutenant," Sandoval said. "And as you've expressed a desire to be useful, I hope you'll recall that I've requested you to make suggestions regarding a route for our overland trek."

"I recall," Valentin said neutrally.

"Thank you, Lieutenant," Sandoval told her. She turned to go.

"Captain," a quiet voice called from behind her.

She turned. Valentin was holding out Sandoval's helmet, weapons belt, and gloves which she had left on the table below the map.

"You've forgotten something. Several somethings, actually." She shook her blonde head in disapproval.

"And if I may say so, this isn't the first time, Captain."

Sandoval looked at the bulky helmet, the constricting gloves, the heavy belt. "You're quite right, Lieutenant," she replied, smiling. "It isn't the first time." Turning her back, she walked decisively from the car.

* * * * *

One hand on the door of the makeshift operating theater, Sandoval hesitated. A pair of booted feet was visible under the solar panels of Number Two MedCenter van. Who had the expertise to repair the solar panels? Crossing to the other van, she rapped on the booted soles.

"Identify yourself," she said crisply. "This is Captain Sandoval."

There was a moment of silence. Then a muffled voice replied, "Solar Tech Four Hart." A pause. "I suppose you'll want me to come down."

Sandoval's eyebrows shot up. Hart — the missing Arizonan. What had persuaded her to return? Surprising little devil. "Are you doing something important, Tech Hart?"

"Dr. Ashe seems to think so," Hart's voice replied. "She told me to get power restored to these vans. The wounded troopers are going to be put in Number Two."

"Carry on with your work," Sandoval told her gruffly. "But stay there when you're finished. I want to talk to you."

"All right," Hart agreed, sounding miserable.

Sandoval chuckled. Poor Hart. No doubt she

110

expected the worst. Well, let her stew awhile. No point in tipping her hand too soon. Mercy had to be judiciously meted out to be appreciated.

* * * * *

"I'm not a practicing physician, you understand," Ashe told Sandoval. "I haven't done this kind of thing for years."

Sandoval looked around, noting that her troopers seemed to be resting comfortably. Rincon's right forearm was bandaged, but she flexed the hand for Sandoval, grinned, and gave her the thumbs-up sign. Johnson, her arm in a sling, sketched a feeble salute. Sandoval nodded to them.

"But as you can see, I managed," Ashe said, crossing her arms and looking at Sandoval. Behind Ashe, a tall young woman in white coveralls cleaned a tray of instruments.

"Good," Sandoval said quietly. "And thank you."

Ashe blinked, clearly taken aback by such civility.

"And the other trooper — Wilkins?"

Ashe shrugged, and motioned Sandoval to the back of the van. There an inert figure lay, fresh sutures in her lower lip, a small bandage on her temple, eyes half closed. "I've fixed the apparent damage," Ashe said. "But we don't have X-ray facilities, of course, and I think she has a concussion. Also —" Ashe paused, running a hand through her hair in frustration. "Because we don't have the facilities to do the tests, I can't tell what she may have been infected with when she was raped."

Sandoval's lips tightened in anger. "Apart from the Red Death, you mean."

111

"Apart from that," Ashe agreed. "I think we should assume she's got it now. Most of these border bandits do."

Sandoval snorted. "Then anything else she might have contracted seems somewhat beside the point, doesn't it, Doctor?"

Ashe nodded, sadness in her eyes. "Yes."

Sandoval gazed out the window at the pine trees on the hillside. "Doctor, I need to have a talk with you."

"Oh? What do you want?" Ashe inquired suspiciously.

Sandoval smiled. "Only some information. In fact, we can trade."

Ashe frowned. "All right," she said, shrugging. "Why don't we go on over to Number Two Van. Medina," she called to the young woman in white, "when you're finished cleaning up, wait for me here. And keep your eye on Wilkins. I want to know if her condition changes."

"All right," Medina said. She looked sidelong at Sandoval, clearly apprehensive. Finally she said, "Captain, may I ask you a question?"

Sandoval shrugged. "Ask."

"Will you punish Hart?"

Sandoval smiled wryly. "For breaking into prison? No."

Medina's expression said that she disapproved of such levity. "Captain, she *did* escape. Surely that's against your regulations."

"It probably is," she said. "But here on the border we have a certain leeway with regulations. Necessity forces us to improvise. But to answer your first question, no, I don't intend to punish Hart."

"Thank you," Medina answered fervently. Then, as if conscious that she had revealed too much, she added, "We need her. She's the only tech we have."

Sandoval smiled. "Hart is fortunate to have such a loyal advocate," she commented, noting how Medina's lovely face reddened in embarrassment.

"She's my friend," Medina admitted. "Friends should be loyal to each other."

"Indeed they should," Sandoval agreed, following Ashe outside.

Sandoval rapped on Hart's boot soles again. "Tech Hart, you may join your friend in the van."

"But —" Hart began.

"It's all right, Hart," Dr. Ashe said. "Captain Sandoval and I have some things to discuss. We'd like privacy. Go help Medina. You can clean up while she attends to Wilkins. Then you can finish your job here."

Hart wormed her way out from under the solar panels, then climbed down the ladder. Brushing off her coveralls, she looked up quickly at Sandoval.

A fox face, Sandoval thought. That dark red hair and those clever gray eyes. Yes, she looks capable of outwitting Lau, or anyone else for that matter. Hart blinked, and Sandoval saw the ghosts of old hurts in her eyes. Another old child, she thought, her heart contracting.

"You harvested my blood without my permission," Hart accused.

Sandoval saw the fear in her eyes, realized that this was hard for her to say, and admired her for it.

"In Arizona, that's a crime." When Sandoval said nothing in return, she continued. "There are a hundred units of RD negative blood in the cooler.

113

Why did you need mine? And if you really did need it, why didn't you *ask*?"

Sandoval tried hard not to smile at such naïveté. "I have orders to deliver the RD negative blood in the cooler to Los Angeles," she told Hart. "That blood is the property of the Republic of California. But two of my troopers are going to need transfusions in a few days. I made the decision to harvest your blood because you're their type. Why didn't I ask?" She tried her best to look fearsome. It wouldn't do to let this young woman think she'd scored a victory. Even though she was right. "Because, Solar Tech Hart, I don't need to ask."

Hart opened her mouth to say something else, but Ashe cut her off. "Enough," Ashe said, casting an apprehensive glance in Sandoval's direction. "Go on back inside, Hart."

With one last reproachful look for Sandoval, Hart went.

"A woman of high moral principles," Sandoval commented. "But rather naïve."

"Oh, I don't know," Ashe disagreed. "She's a trifle ignorant of the ways of the world, but that's nothing to be ashamed of. Ignorance can be cured. A healthy dose of reality usually does it."

Sandoval opened the door to the empty van and motioned Ashe inside. "Sit down, please," she invited. "You must be tired."

Ashe sat heavily on one of the folding seats. Sandoval took another, and they looked at each other from across the van.

"Thank you again for attending to my troopers," Sandoval said.

114

Ashe studied Sandoval's face for a long moment. Sadly, Sandoval realized that here was a woman with whom she might have been friends had circumstances been different. A woman of courage and principles. A woman like she herself had once been, she thought bleakly.

"You're welcome," Ashe told her.

"I want to make a pact with you," Sandoval said. Realizing how warm it was in the van, she reached up and unbuttoned her collar.

"Go on," Ashe said.

"I'd like to discuss my orders with you, Doctor. And I'll acknowledge before we start that I'm committing treason." She fixed Ashe with an appraising look. "So now you have a weapon to use against me if you choose."

Ashe raised her eyebrows. "Why take the risk?"

"Because there are some questions I need answered. And I believe the answers may be vital to our well-being." She frowned. "Too many things about this mission don't . . . feel right."

"What makes you think I have any information you might need?" Ashe asked.

Sandoval paused. "Because you're a virologist. My orders have to do with the Red Death."

Ashe cocked her head to one side. "Continue."

Sandoval stretched her feet out in front of her, legs crossed at the ankles. She was unsure how to proceed. Ashe could be a valuable ally, or a stubborn, intractable foe. "What do you know about the progress of the Red Death in California, Doctor?"

Ashe shook her head. "Virtually nothing. We've tried repeatedly to contact the authorities there, but

115

with no success. Until last month. Then — largely because we had something concrete to offer them — our overtures were accepted."

"Indeed they were," Sandoval agreed. "And for a very good reason. The truth is, Doctor, we're losing the fight against the Red Death. The plan of the Provisional Government — to keep a donor pool in order to transfuse administrative and military personnel, and to let the virus burn itself out among the general populace — just isn't working. We've had hundreds of thousands of deaths, and the disease shows no signs of weakening. Also, the donor pool is getting smaller."

Sandoval grimaced. "Tell me, is it true that you've developed a viable vaccine? We've heard only rumors about this."

Ashe ran a hand through her hair. "An experimental vaccine. It's not made from killed virus, though, so it makes a lot of people sick." Seeing the puzzlement on Sandoval's face, she paused. "How much chemistry do you know, Captain?"

"Not much," Sandoval admitted. "I studied literature and philosophy in college. But I did take a general science course or two."

Ashe looked at her in amazement. "Philosophy? And this is what you've come to?" She shook her head. "Never mind. Forgive me if I lecture, but if you're to understand the vaccine, you'll have to understand the virus."

"I'd like that," Sandoval said. "It never hurts to know more about one's enemy."

Ashe took a deep breath. "Back when we had the facilities to study viruses, even then there was disagreement among scientists as to whether viruses

116

were living organisms. You see, as long as they're outside living cells, they're inert. They don't synthesize proteins, they don't generate metabolic energy, and they don't reproduce."

Sandoval raised her eyebrows. "What are they, then, if they're not living organisms?"

Ashe shook her head. "No one knows. Structurally, they're quite simple — packets of nucleic acid surrounded by protective protein coats."

"That sounds innocuous enough."

"It does, doesn't it?" Ashe agreed. "But once a virus infects living cells, the trouble starts. It injects its nucleic acid into the cell and turns it into a virus-producing factory. Somehow it commandeers the synthesizing mechanism of the cell, stopping normal functions, and causing synthesis of the new virus instead. After a large number of viruses have been produced, the infected cell bursts, or passes the viruses out through the cell membrane. Then the process begins again."

"Formidable." Sandoval commented, impressed. "An invading army that continually makes more invaders. A perfect battle plan."

"It is," Ashe agreed. "I've never thought of it quite like that before, but it's a neat analogy."

"How does a vaccine work against viruses? They sound unstoppable."

"They are — almost," Ashe said. "Developing antiviral agents has always been difficult because agents that are harmful to viruses are also likely to injure host cells. But at the turn of the century a lot of progress was made in the chemical synthesis of antiviral agents, so we began to understand more about the development of antiviral vaccines. Well, in

117

simple terms, the vaccine — which is usually made from a part of the virus's protein coat — is injected into the body where it produces antibodies. These antibodies are specialized proteins which combine with the virus to render it inactive."

"An elegant process," Sandoval said. "The virus becomes the agent of its own destruction."

Ashe laughed. "Yes, the process is elegant. But finding a vaccine to combat the Red Death made me lose my appreciation for the aesthetics of biochemistry, I'm afraid."

"Oh? Why so?"

Ashe looked at Sandoval speculatively. "One thing you may not know is that the Red Death was a product of genetic engineering. Do you know what that is?"

"More or less," Sandoval said. "An organism is altered in the laboratory in order to fulfill some specific purpose."

"Good enough," Ashe said. "In the case of the Red Death, a relatively innocuous virus was selected. Then it was altered in several ways — the most important being the time required to commandeer the facilities of the host cell. This new virus — the so-called Red Death virus — requires almost no time at all to do its work. The first infected host cells literally explode within hours of infection. Then the process continues at an exponentially rising rate. Yes," Ashe mused, "the organism was tailor-made to produce an epidemic. No doubt about it. But it might not have been so successful had its creators not understood American sociology as well as they did."

Sandoval was puzzled. "Sociology? What did that have to do with it?"

Ashe raised an eyebrow. "It had everything to do with it. If the young studs of the 'nineties hadn't been so obsessed with screwing, the virus might have been controlled. The HIV vaccine had one unfortunate sociological effect — it gave the green light to sexual promiscuity. Pent-up demand and all that." Ashe looked at Sandoval, her brows drawn together in a frown. "Making the Red Death a sexually transmitted disease was a stroke of genius. Diabolical genius."

Sandoval grunted. She had never thought about the Red Death in quite this way before. "What you say makes sense — it *was* diabolical. Yet with so much working against you, you were successful in finding a vaccine."

"An experimental vaccine," Ashe emphasized. "It's killed people, Captain. It needs refinement. And I have to admit that its discovery came about largely by accident. I knew what I intended to do. I had a plan mapped out. But I wasn't very hopeful."

"Why not?"

"You see, what we had working against us was the fact that the Red Death is an exceptionally complex virus. It contains well over five hundred genes. The largest number yet recorded in a virus." She looked away. "It was daunting. But we started in, hoping for a break. It took us six months to get organized, then at the end of eighteen months of work, we were dumbfounded to discover that we had created an antivirus that was successful. Some of the time, anyway. We'd be far better off with a vaccine from the killed virus, but this works. As I said, it's highly experimental, and certainly needs testing, but it does work."

"Fascinating," Sandoval commented. "But why

doesn't all of North America know about your results?"

Ashe raised an eyebrow. "You tell me. We let the United Nations Red Death Task Force know about the vaccine five months ago."

"And?"

"They're still studying it."

"Don't you think that's odd?"

"Yes, I do," Ashe agreed. "There would seem to be little time to waste. It's almost as if —"

"As if what, Doctor?" Sandoval asked quietly.

"As if the results were being suppressed." Ashe shook her head. "But that's insane, of course."

"I wonder . . ." Sandoval said. She was silent for a moment. Should she really share her suspicions with Ashe? Since she had first read her orders she had thought that kidnapping the Arizonan virologist was running an unconscionable risk. The Provisional Government had few facilities for Red Death research. As did BioStrike Central. And what if something were to happen to Ashe en route to headquarters? Her knowledge of the vaccine would perish with her. No, Sandoval had thought, far better for the course of the Red Death to leave Dr. Ashe in Tucson. "Doctor, by now you know I was ordered to kidnap you. To bring you and your team to BioStrike Central. It seems as though the California Provisional Government wants you."

Ashe nodded. "So I surmised."

"That seems a rather foolish enterprise, don't you think?"

Ashe blinked. "I'm biased, of course," she commented wryly, "but that thought had occurred to me."

120

Sandoval looked at Ashe. She has the same suspicions I do, she realized. Only her perception of me as an enemy prevents her from confiding in me. "Tell me, Doctor," she said, "what was the purpose of your mission, as far as you knew it?"

"To see that the thirty units of lyophilized vaccine in the MedCenter van were delivered into the proper hands."

Sandoval was not surprised. She had been earlier, when a search of the MedCenter vans had turned up the vaccine. Her orders had mentioned nothing about this. She wondered whether she was to assume the vaccine to be contraband and seize it. But why had no mention been made of the vaccine in her orders? It was surely far more valuable than anything else on the train. "Into whose hands were you to deliver the vaccine?" Sandoval asked.

Ashe looked at Sandoval, comprehension evident in her eyes. "Captain, it seems that someone on this train has orders that supercede yours." She rubbed a hand over her face. "I'm far too tired to try to make sense of all this. Wheels within wheels may delight philosophers, but I have no patience with such things." She turned her clear blue eyes on Sandoval. "It seems I have to trust someone. My common sense warns me it shouldn't be you."

Sandoval said nothing.

Ashe looked at her. "Did you euthanize those men?" Ashe asked softly.

Sandoval was surprised at the question. "No," she said. "Corporal Lujan and I took them into the desert and pointed them toward home. They had survival packs from your own vans. I gave Collins — the tech driver — the drug you provided. Cyanide, wasn't it?

121

And a gun. They can make their own choices. Murdering the innocent was never one of my favorite activities."

Ashe shook her head. "My God," she said. "You're full of surprises, aren't you?"

Sandoval met her gaze, wondering briefly just what Ashe thought of her. A killer with a heart? A philosopher-murderer?

"I'm going to trust you," Ashe said after a moment. "Common sense might dictate otherwise, but something in my gut tells me I'm right about you. Very well, Captain. I'll tell you what you want to know. I was to deliver the vaccine to your junior officer."

"You must be mistaken," Sandoval said. "I have no junior officer."

Ashe looked puzzled. "You haven't? But that's all I know. I was told to give the vaccine to your lieutenant."

Sandoval felt her blood pressure rise by about fifty points. "To my *lieutenant?* Were you given a name?"

"Yes," Ashe said, "a European-sounding name. But I'm sorry to say that in all the excitement, I've forgotten —"

"Valentin," Sandoval said through clenched teeth. "It's Lieutenant Valentin, isn't it?"

"Yes," Ashe said, nodding. "Lieutenant Valentin. That's it."

* * * * *

Sandoval stood at the edge of the flatbed, looking down into the ravine. Behind her, Hart, Medina, and

122

Dr. Ashe, assisted by two of Sandoval's troopers, were busy moving the wounded to the recovery van. Sandoval stared unseeing at the scenery, her mind preoccupied with a jumble of thoughts of Lieutenant Valentin, BioStrike Central, her orders, the vaccine, the Red Death, and the women on the train. As the train chugged around the flank of the mountain, the late afternoon sun caught Sandoval full in the eyes. She realized that she had eaten nothing all day.

She decided abruptly to invite Lieutenant Valentin to share her evening meal. She would charm Valentin, put her at ease. Smiling, she put her hands on her hips, then, sensing something was wrong, looked around quickly. Her weapons belt. She had left it behind in the command car. Was she becoming careless, she wondered, assuming that the Arizonans and Ashe were no longer a threat? It was true that she felt safer with them than she did with Valentin. And although she certainly couldn't wear her weapons to dinner, she would make certain that Lujan was nearby, and armed. And she would tell Lujan what to expect. That should be good enough. She chuckled.

The cat-and-mouse aspects of the plan appealed to her. She didn't believe for one moment that Valentin was more devious or clever than she. She'd trick Valentin into disclosing what she wanted to know — she was certain of that. And then she would arrest her. With Valentin out of commission, Sandoval intended to look through the Lieutenant's belongings, including the SunRaycer in which she had so ostentatiously arrived. Sandoval was willing to bet that the answer to the question of Lieutenant Valentin would be a very interesting one indeed.

She moved back from the edge of the flatbed and

turned to make her way to the next-to-last car. Stepping onto the platform between the cars, she rapped on the door, waiting for the trooper inside to open it. After a moment, the door slid back and Sandoval strode through into the car.

A score of faces turned her way, faces framed by blonde hair and brown, red hair and black. Women in blue shirts, in gray shirts, in pants, in flowered skirts, turned and looked up at her as she picked a way through to the door at the far end of the car. The faces turned to follow her like sunflowers, and for no reason she could name, she looked back. Instantly she knew she had made a mistake. The faces, she thought, the faces. Each was unique. Distinct. And the eyes. Each pair of eyes had a message for her alone — hope, fear, accusation, despair. And today, for some reason, she heard them. All the messages, all the souls' cries. She heard every one. She blinked, suddenly overcome. So many eyes. So many faces. So many responsibilities. She shuddered, digging her nails into her palms, willing self control. Only dignity prevented her from pushing the women roughly aside and running from the car. Forcing herself to see nothing but the door at the end of the car, she began walking mechanically forward. One more step, she told herself. One more step.

Suddenly, violently, she was thrown to the floor. Women cried out. She heard the screaming of metal as the train's brakes were applied, and the car beneath her groaned and shook like a beast in pain. There must be something on the tracks, she thought. Villanova would never brake like that for any other reason.

"Brace yourselves!" Sandoval shouted to the confused, shouting women. But her warning went unheeded. She had time only to roll into a ball and cover her head before the train, with a terrible shrieking of metal on metal, ran solidly into whatever obstacle blocked its way. Sandoval was catapulted across the floor, and as the car tilted and the floor became a wall, she struck the new vertical surface with enough force to make her cry out. Then she tumbled with a score of other women into a heap. She fell on someone, someone fell on her, and she was afraid she might suffocate. The car shifted again, and something hit the back of her head with the sound of an axe hitting wood. A starburst went off behind her eyes, and as she fell into it, she realized what had happened. My God, she thought in terror — we've jumped the tracks. We're going over the edge!

CHAPTER 7

*The prologues are over. It is a question, now
of final belief. . . . It is a time to choose.*
                    Wallace Stevens, *Asides on the Oboe*

Hart picked herself up from the dirt at the side of
the tracks and brushed off her coveralls with hands
that still shook. She might have been killed, she
realized. They all might have been killed had it not
been for the fact that the vehicles car had broken
loose from the rest of the train after the first violent
application of the brakes. She, Ashe, and two

126

BioStrike troopers had been outside the vans at the time and had been thrown off the flatbed into the dirt. Fortunately, none of them was seriously hurt.

Kneeling at the side of the tracks, Hart watched in horrified fascination as the train's cars, joined together like beads on a string, crashed through the trees on their way down the steep incline. Beside her, Ashe watched in evident horror. The two BioStrike troopers, looking every bit as dazed and shaken as she felt, rose unsteadily to their feet.

"Madre de Dios!" one of them said softly. "It looks like a broken toy."

Hart scrambled to her feet. There, fifty feet below her, the train's cars had come to rest on their sides among the trees. Most were still joined together — these had not been able to slide very far down the forested hillside. But two of the cars had been torn from each other, and their shattered remains could be seen far down the steep hillside. Hart swallowed. Could anyone have survived such a thing?

"The Captain!" exclaimed the younger of the two troopers. "She was in the last car!" She flung her helmet to the ground, unbuckled her weapons belt, and without another word, began to descend the slope.

"Wait!" Ashe called after her. "The cars haven't settled yet. They may slide farther."

The trooper hesitated, turning to look at Ashe. With her helmet and weapons off, Hart saw that she had suddenly become human — a young, slim, sun-browned woman, with expressive dark eyes, and crisply curling black hair. Hart was shocked. *Why, she's no older than I am. She could be a vehicles tech — they wear black coveralls. She looks just like one of*

127

us. Hart shivered. What was the matter with her? She should be thinking of how alien the BioStrike troopers were, not how human.

"We shouldn't wait," the trooper said. "The cars may go right on down over the edge. Then it will be too late. We have to act now." She looked up at Hart. "You're not hurt. Will you help me?"

Hart looked around. Ashe stood leaning heavily on a trooper's shoulder, favoring an ankle. The trooper was bleeding from a cut over her eye, cradling her right wrist in her left hand, wincing in pain. Hart closed her eyes, feeling the fear hum in her head.

"Please," the trooper begged. "We need to find the Captain."

Faintly, from far down the hillside, Hart heard the cries of women in pain. "I'm coming," she said, keenly aware of how dry her mouth was. "Will you be all right here?" Hart asked Ashe.

"Yes, yes," Ashe said, waving her away. "We'll clean up the mess in the vans. And get ready for the onslaught. Go on. But be careful, for God's sake."

* * * * *

"How do you know your Captain's down there?" Hart asked the young trooper as they proceeded down the hill, digging in their heels, clinging to low-hanging tree branches.

"I had just left the car," she said. "Captain Sandoval was standing in the middle of those Gaia women. I'm sure she's still with them."

They hit a clear spot and the trooper's feet slid out from under her. She began to slide, and Hart took a firmer grip on the branch she was holding and made a grab for the trooper's shirt.

"Thanks," the trooper said, digging her heels in hard. She looked up the slope at Hart. "I'm Corporal Lujan."

"I'm Solar Tech Hart," she said.

"Oh," Lujan answered, recognition in her eyes. *"That* Hart."

Hart looked at her curiously, then continued her descent. They slid down the slope in silence for a few minutes, grabbing onto rocks and trees to slow themselves, stopping every now and then to get their bearings.

"It's getting steeper," Hart commented. "And there are bound to be dozens of wounded. How will we ever get them back up the hill?"

"We won't," Lujan said. "We'll haul them out of the car, do what we can, and leave them for the rest of the troopers. But Captain Sandoval —" Lujan's voice broke, and Hart looked over at her, astonished at the depth of the young woman's feelings. "I won't leave her," Lujan said. "I'll bring her up myself." She released her hold on a low branch and slid the remaining few feet to the railway car.

Too surprised to speak, Hart followed her. Could she be wrong about Captain Sandoval? Anyone able to command that sort of impassioned loyalty couldn't be the cold, cruel sadist Hart had imagined. She frowned. This was all too confusing.

The car had come to rest on its side, against two enormous pine trees. It had splintered one of them, and the top of that tree had, in turn, toppled onto the railway car, breaking it in two. Evidently the car's descent had almost pushed the second tree completely off the cliff, for it hung at an impossible angle, roots in the air, seemingly connected to the soil by only a prayer. Hart winced. The lower half of the bisected car lay against the tree's roots, and even as she watched, the tree shivered in the grip of gravity, and the car slid closer to the edge.

Lujan cried out, and gripped the broken plank walls as if to prevent the car's falling. She would have vaulted up onto the sloping, splintered boards if Hart hadn't held her back.

"No," Hart said. "It's too unstable. Lift me up over there. I'm lighter than you. I can look through the window."

Lujan hesitated, then nodded. "You're right. Come on, then." She bent over, lacing her hands together. Hart placed one foot in Lujan's hands, a hand on her back, and Lujan straightened up. Hart put both hands tentatively on the car's side and peered through the window. Before she could help herself, a cry of horror escaped her lips.

"What is it?" Lujan shouted, almost dropping Hart. "Is it Captain Sandoval?"

"No," Hart said after a moment. "It isn't." The dead faces of Eda and Cora stared up at her, along with half a dozen women from the Gaians' car. All dead. They had to be, she told herself. They looked so . . . broken. And there was so much blood. Suddenly the car shifted under her hands. "Lujan, let me down!" she yelled. "The car's going over!"

She hit the ground with enough force to throw her backwards. With terrified disbelief she watched her booted feet slide toward the railway car, felt

130

herself oozing down the slope after it. "No!" she cried out, twisting her body, scrabbling at the earth.

Lujan shouted something unintelligible, and then her strong hands grabbed Hart's. "Just hang on!" Lujan called again. "I've got you!"

Below her, Hart heard the broken car go over the edge. The pine tree finally gave way with a snapping of branches and rending of roots, and the remains of the car slid over the edge. Suddenly there was silence. Then, after a moment, a crash from somewhere far below.

Hart sobbed, kicked, and finally drove her toes into the hillside. Holding tightly to Lujan's hands, she pulled herself up beside her. Lujan put an arm around her, and she collapsed against the trooper, sick with fear. "I'm sorry," she apologized to Lujan. "The car was full of dead women. I knew some of them. They were kind to me."

Lujan squeezed Hart's shoulder briefly. "It's all right," she said. "No one ever gets used to the sight of death." After a moment she took her arm from Hart's shoulder. "Well, that leaves the other half of the car. Ready to try again?"

Hart nodded, although it was the last thing in the world she wanted to do.

"This half looks pretty solid," Lujan said, thumping it with her fist. "I think it's well braced against the tree. I'll climb in through the window."

"Lujan," Hart said diffidently.

Lujan turned to look at her. "What?"

"Don't you think . . ." She trailed off, unable to complete the thought. "Nothing," she said, shaking her head. Lujan shrugged and turned away. Hart swallowed, afraid of what they might find. Suddenly she wanted very much for Sandoval to be alive. But common sense told her the Captain must be dead. However, it came over her, watching Lujan straighten up, leap onto the wheels, then haul herself up the broken boards and through the shattered window, that the trooper had to do this. It was important to her; she had to try. Is this what it means to be brave, Hart asked herself, to make an attempt even when you know it's likely to be futile? To do the right thing even if it means putting yourself at risk? She felt a wave of admiration for Lujan. Are they all this brave, these BioStrike troopers, she asked herself. Or is it only Lujan? Dammit, she thought in despair, who are these women? I want to hate them. All of them. And Sandoval most of all.

"Hart!" Lujan called. "I've found her!"

* * * * *

Hart was convinced that they dragged Sandoval the last fifteen feet up the hillside by sheer force of will. Their hands were skinned and bloody from grabbing rocks and branches; the elbows of their shirts and the knees of their pants were worn through. They were so exhausted they could hardly crawl. Still, they pulled Sandoval along between them, Lujan alternately talking to Sandoval, then cursing under her breath in Spanish, Hart sobbing unashamedly when she had breath for it. Finally the top of the hill came in sight, and two pairs of blackshirted BioStrike arms reached down to take the Captain from them.

"Take her to Dr. Ashe," Hart croaked. "She'll know what to do."

"Corporal, do you want —" one of the troopers asked.

"Go on, Lau!" Lujan said roughly. "Do it! We'll be all right."

Then they were left alone.

Lujan rolled to one knee, groaned, then pulled herself upright. She reached a hand down to Hart.

Gingerly, Hart extended her own hand, wincing at the raw places as Lujan helped her stand. "Your Captain will be all right," she told Lujan. "She answered you once or twice. That's a good sign."

"Do you think so?" Lujan asked.

"Yes, I do," Hart said earnestly. "And Ashe is a good doctor. She's Tucson MedCenter's best," she elaborated, realizing how important this was to Lujan. "Come on, let's go on up to the MedCenter vans ourselves. We have to get these cuts cleaned up or we're going to be no good to anyone."

Lujan nodded, and allowed Hart to lead her over to the flatbed. They climbed aboard, and Hart gasped. Women were sitting or lying in groups around the MedCenter vans, bleeding, holding heads, arms, wrists. Hart did a quick count. There must have been twenty wounded waiting for Dr. Ashe. Hart saw a medtech and a BioStrike trooper moving through the groups, instructing some of them to move closer to the vans, and moving some farther away. Triage, Hart realized. She wondered briefly where Medina was.

"Listen," Hart told Lujan. "We don't need to take up the medical personnel's time. We'll go on into that van, the gray one that says Service. It was mine. We'll use the first aid kit."

"All right," Lujan said. "But then I need to see the Captain. Can you get me through that mess?"

"Yes," she said. "I think I can get you through."

Lujan relaxed visibly.

"Let's clean up now," Hart said, opening the van door and rummaging around for her hastily discarded survival pack. Even though the contents had not been put back in their proper places, at least she had remembered to put it back in the Service van. Her gaze slid across the floor to the space underneath Collins' seat where she had stashed the pistol. Although it was there and loaded, it didn't make her feel safe. Not any more. Anxious, she handed half the first aid supplies to Lujan. "Here," she said. "Some of these cuts are pretty deep, but we'll just have to do the best we can. I don't think Dr. Ashe will be done with the serious cases for hours."

Lujan dabbed away at her cuts. "Be careful of this," she said, holding up a cotton ball.

"Be careful of what?"

Lujan looked at Hart shamefacedly. "Of my blood," she said through gritted teeth. "Don't get it in your open cuts. Last year I helped the medic stitch up some of our troopers. I was careless. Now I'm RD positive."

"You don't know, do you?" Hart asked.

"Know what?"

"All the Arizonans have been vaccinated. We can't get the Red Death."

Lujan blinked. "Oh," she said, brown eyes wide. Then she looked away. "I envy you, Hart," she said quietly, dabbing at her hands. "To think that there's finally a vaccine, but that it's too late for me." She

134

grimaced. "Oh well. We don't have a long life expectancy here on the border anyhow."

"I'm sorry," Hart said lamely.

"Tell me something," Lujan said after a moment. "Why did you agree to help me? You can't have very good feelings about us. After all, we kidnapped you. And I was the one who tasered you. You could just have easily let me go down there alone."

Hart shrugged. "I just did what anyone would have done."

Lujan took a deep breath. "Before this crash, I never even talked to any of the donors we rounded up. I didn't want to." She looked at Hart intently. "Maybe I was afraid if I did, I wouldn't be able to do my job. Maybe I was afraid they might be human. Like you."

Hart swallowed, aware that Lujan was trying to tell her something very important. "And now?"

Lujan laughed softly, bitterly. "I don't know. I owe my life a dozen times over to Captain Sandoval. I owe her for taking me out of prison three years ago. I can't be disloyal to her."

Hart frowned, wanting to understand. "Do all the troopers feel about her the way you do?"

Lujan smiled shyly, a quick flash of white teeth in her brown face. "Yes. She picked every one of us herself. And she's given us something we never had before — self-respect."

"But she picked you to kidnap people like me," Hart said quietly.

Lujan hung her head. "I know. But, Hart, things are too complicated for someone like me to be able to figure out. The Red Death, what's going to happen to

California, to America — hell, I have no idea what the world was like before I became a BioStrike trooper. I can scarcely remember what my neighborhood was like."

"But —" Hart began, then broke off. Who was she to tell this young woman anything? She, too, could hardly remember her former life. Reality for her had become Tucson MedCenter — the elite club formed for those fortunate enough to have escaped the Red Death. "I know what you mean," she told Lujan. "I used to think we were doing the right thing at Tucson MedCenter — keeping our blood pure — but now I'm not so sure."

"You know what I think?" Lujan said, laying her head against the wall of the van and closing her eyes. "The only thing in the world worth stirring an inch for is love. It's sure the only thing worth dying for." She opened her eyes. "I think about dying a lot, Hart. Why not — I won't be Stage One forever. And sometimes . . . I feel like a walking dead woman." She bit her lip. "Even the condemned are entitled to one last wish. But not me. Do you know what my final request would be, Hart?"

Hart shook her head.

Lujan closed her eyes. "To hold a woman in my arms again. To have her hold me. To kiss her." She shook her head. "But I couldn't. I'd kill her." The cotton with which Lujan had been swabbing her cuts fell from her fingers. "I'm too tired to do any more of this," she mumbled. "I should find out the status of the Unit. And the condition of the Captain. But . . ." Her head fell to one side, and she crumbled sideways.

Hart caught her, and laid her down on the van

floor. She took Lujan's hands in hers and finished
cleaning out her cuts, wincing as the peroxide
bubbled in the deeper ones. Then she put a blanket
under Lujan's head. She brushed the curly hair off
Lujan's forehead, and with one finger traced a small
white scar beside Lujan's mouth. "You wouldn't kill
me," she murmured, and bending over, brushed
Lujan's lips with her own.

Lujan stirred a little. "Hart," she whispered,
clearly more unconscious than awake.

"I'm here," Hart said. She kissed Lujan again, a
little more firmly this time, then sat up.

"You . . . will you check on the Captain?"

"Okay."

Lujan reached for Hart's hand, squeezed it, then
let it fall.

Hart felt her face grow hot with embarrassment.
What on earth had possessed her to kiss Lujan? Hart
got one knee under her and pushed herself upright.
Her elbows and knees felt as though they were on
fire, and the muscles in her arms trembled and hurt
so much she could hardly lift a hand to open the van
door. She looked back once at Lujan, then closed the
door behind her as quietly as she could.

* * * * *

The scene at the MedCenter vans seemed to Hart
to be a picture of hell. Several large fires had been
set beside the tracks, and many smaller ones burned
in metal containers on the flatbed. Their light was
insufficient to work by, but it was adequate to see
the dead. With a surge of anger Hart saw that the
bodies had simply been left where they lay. No one

137

had covered them. No one had even closed their eyes. Horrified, she realized that this outer ring of women, the ones she now stood among, had only an hour earlier been alive. They had been triaged as the ones least likely to survive, had received no attention, and had died. Hart looked around. There must be a dozen women lying here. All dead. So when someone pulled at Hart's pantleg, she cried aloud in fright.

"Water," the woman begged feebly.

Hart looked down. It was a BioStrike trooper, one side of her head clotted with dark blood, her nose broken, both eyes swollen shut.

"Water," she whispered, weaker this time, one hand raised in supplication.

Hart knelt, looking around for a container of water, a canteen. Anything. But there was nothing close by. Of course there wouldn't be, she thought grimly. Precious resources shouldn't be wasted on the dying. It's only practical. She took the woman in her arms. "Sorry," she told her. "Sorry."

"Will I make it?" the trooper whispered.

"Sure you will," Hart answered, seeing no harm in the lie. "You'll be fine."

"Good," the trooper whispered. Then, with a sigh, she went limp in Hart's arms.

Because she couldn't think of anything else to do, Hart held the trooper for a moment longer. She wanted to cry, but was too tired for any more emotion. Gently, she laid the trooper on the dusty board floor.

"Shocking, isn't it?" a voice said at her elbow. "So many wasted lives."

Hart turned around. A young, blonde BioStrike trooper knelt there, helmetless, the firelight turning

138

her hair to flame. But though her words were compassionate, her tone respectful, her eyes seemed alight with something dark and gleeful. Hart felt the hair rise on the back of her neck. Had she been standing, she would have turned and run. As it was, she simply stared.

The woman shifted position a little, and the firelight behind her made a copper nimbus of her hair. Suddenly, Hart thought of the madwoman Irena. Hair-on-fire she had called Hart. The angel of death. Hart was suddenly convinced that Irena's angel was here.

"I'm Lieutenant Valentin," the woman said.

Hart swallowed, unable for a moment to speak. Then she nodded. Some acknowledgement had to be made. "I'm Solar Tech Hart." She noted in astonishment that the woman's uniform was impeccable. Every crease was knife-edged. Even her boots gleamed. Clearly Lieutenant Valentin had not been taking part in the rescue operation.

The lieutenant nodded. "I know who you are. I came to introduce myself. You see, I'm in command now."

Shocked, Hart searched the woman's face.

"But, Captain Sandoval . . . that is, we —"

The lieutenant shook her head. "We lost her, I'm afraid."

Hart was stunned into silence. "Lost her?" she whispered finally. "You mean, she *died*?"

Valentin nodded, eyes downcast.

Hart was shocked to discover how bereft she felt. The woman she had regarded as her personal persecutor, a superhuman being, had been reduced to mortal status. Death had leveled her, as it had leveled

everyone else on those ill-fated cars. As it would level
her, too. She shivered, wanting the certainty of this
vision to pass. Never before had she been so cowed
by the thought of her own mortality. Captain
Sandoval, she whispered silently. We needed you.
Lujan was right.

"I need your help, Tech Hart," the lieutenant said
earnestly.

Hart looked up dully. "I have to go and find Dr.
Ashe. She'll need me. I'm not hurt. I can be a lot of
help to her."

"I've spoken to Dr. Ashe," Valentin said. "She
agrees that I need you more than she does. She
wants you to come with me."

"Oh," Hart said, surprised and disappointed that
Ashe didn't need her. "But —"

Valentin drew her pistol and pointed it at Hart's
head. "I have no time for persuasion," she said
through clenched teeth. "Up, Solar Tech Hart."

Stunned, Hart stood up.

"Into the woods," Valentin said, gesturing with
her pistol.

Hart jumped down from the flatbed and, followed
by Valentin, walked into the woods.

"These fires will bring every bandit for ten
miles," Valentin muttered. "If we're to get away from
here, we have to act now."

"How can we possibly get away?" Hart asked
sarcastically. "Most of the women can't even walk."

Valentin came forward to walk beside Hart, and
patted her encouragingly on the shoulder. "That's
why I need you," she said. "And I'm sorry I had to
pull my gun to make my point. Are you familiar with
electronics?" she asked.

140

Hart shrugged. "Some. It depends on what we're talking about."

"We're talking about this," Valentin said, switching the beam of her light to illuminate a wider area. It picked out the bulky shapes of the OLVs and then a sleek, black bullet-shaped vehicle with an array of energy panels on the roof. Hart walked forward excitedly. This must be the vehicle on the flatbed that had been covered by the heavy canvas tarp! She put a hand on its cool, metallic fender.

"What is it?" she asked in awe.

"The SunRaycer," Valentin said proudly. "A prototype vehicle. A gift to the BioStrike Force from a friendly international power."

"From a . . ." Hart found herself too amazed to continue.

Valentin laughed. "You find it so surprising that a foreign power has taken an interest in California?"

"Yes," Hart said frankly. "We heard that the Red Death was out of control in California. And that the United Nations won't even consider lifting its quarantine on America until it's brought under control. That's what the Commonwealth Task Force is going to California to investigate. At least," she stammered, "that's what I thought."

"Well," Valentin said mysteriously, "there are other ways to achieve the same ends. The Provisional Government in Los Angeles has botched the handling of the Red Death problem right from the beginning. Fortunately, the BioStrike Forces have their own friends." She looked at Hart speculatively. "You seem to be interested in more than solar cells. Commendable."

Hart tried hard not to be flattered.

"Come over here," Valentin said, lifting the plexiglass bubble that formed the car's roof. Hinged on the rear side, it hissed pneumatically as Valentin lifted. "Step inside," she told Hart.

Awkwardly, Hart slid into the driver's seat.

"The ignition button is there on the dash by your knee," Valentin said. "Push it."

Hart did so. Nothing happened. She looked at Valentin.

"I've checked out the ignition system," Valentin said. "The trouble must be in the collectors."

"Or the wiring between the ignition and the collectors," Hart said, looking at the SunRaycer critically. "This seems to be a hard-wired model. Not too much computerized circuitry."

Valentin grunted. "Can you fix it?"

Hart stepped out of the vehicle. "Maybe. If I could see. And if I had my tools."

Valentin reached into the back of the car and dropped a canvas bag at Hart's feet. "I took the liberty of removing this from your van."

Hart glared at Valentin. "It seems you've thought of everything."

Valentin holstered her gun and gripped Hart's shoulders tightly. "I'm sorry I had to use this," she apologized. "It was really only to get your attention. Now listen to me. Our only hope of getting out of here is this vehicle. Someone has to get to the next BioStrike outpost, report this terrible accident, and tell them where to send help. And how much of it to send. The OLVs are too loud. Everyone from here to Los Angeles would know we're coming. Hart, we're depending on you. Do you understand?"

Unfortunately, it made sense. "I understand," she said. "But I'd feel better if I'd talked to Dr. Ashe."

Valentin sighed, and putting two fingers under Hart's chin, tilted her face up. "You're hurt that she doesn't need you. Isn't that it? And you're also angry with me that I used my gun."

Embarrassed, Hart nodded. Valentin was right on both counts.

"Ashe has troopers helping her move the bodies, and medtechs helping her fix them. She knows that your specialized knowledge can best be used here. Does that make you feel better?"

Hart swallowed. "Yes."

"I'm very sorry about the gun," Valentin said. "I'm not a tactful person. And tonight has been hard on all of us."

"All right," Hart told her, her reluctance diminishing.

Valentin brushed Hart's face with the back of her hand. "Thank you," she said softly. She turned and closed the SunRaycer's hinged roof, motioning Hart toward the energy panels. "I'll hold the light," she said. "Just tell me which tools you need. I'll pass them to you."

* * * * *

It took Hart an hour to find the problem, and two additional hours to repair it. In the crash, several of the wires which connected the storage batteries to the ignition had been severed. But finding the problem meant taking the seats out of the SunRaycer and laboriously tracing the wires where they ran in a

143

channel under the floor. Finally, however, she found the break, and repaired it. Valentin helped her lift the seats back in and bolt them in place. As she turned the last screw, the sun rose.

"You must be exhausted," Valentin said, lifting the roof and motioning Hart inside the car. "Why don't you sit here while I try the ignition."

Gratefully, Hart slumped in the passenger seat.

Valentin stepped into the SunRaycer's driver's seat. She pressed the ignition button. With a reassuring hum, the lights on the dash glowed into life.

"You've got an onboard computer!" Hart exclaimed. "What's that on the screen?"

"It's a topographical map of this area," Valentin said. "The computer also has an ordinary road map in its memory banks. Would you like to see where we are?"

"Oh, yes," Hart said.

Valentin smiled, her face an unearthly green in the phosphor glow. "Press this key here," Valentin said. "Now, type in AERIAL LOCATE."

Hart did so, and a dizzying array of topographical maps flashed across the screen. "It's like flying," Hart exclaimed. Finally the simulated flight stopped.

"We're here," Valentin said, tapping a glowing dot on the screen. "The cliff is over here, and the mountain pass where we were headed is here."

Hart nodded. "I see it," she said. "It's so close. We almost made it."

Valentin sighed. "Yes. We almost did." She looked sidelong at Hart. "Where's your medtag?"

Hart looked down at the front of her coveralls. "Oh," she said, patting a pocket. "Here."

144

"Fine," Valentin said. "But clip it back on, will you?"

"Okay," Hart said. "But why?"

"Because we're going to the nearest BioStrike outpost," Valentin told her, "and I want you to do everything right."

Hart blinked. "Okay," she repeated, wanting to ask questions, but not wanting Valentin to see how nervous this prospect made her.

Valentin put a hand on Hart's knee. "Listen," she said. "When we get where we're going, I intend to plead your case to my superior officer. You may have to go on to Central to speak for yourself, but I don't think there will be any problem in returning you and your fellow Arizonans to Tucson. And in clearing up any difficulties there. Captain Sandoval was wrong to have done what she did. We're not kidnappers, Hart."

Hart's eyes filled with tears.

"There's a change afoot in the BioStrike Forces," Valentin said. "The old guard is being ousted. People like Captain Sandoval simply aren't fit to command any longer. There's a new day dawning for California. For America, too." She paused, clearly considering her next words. "Young people like you shouldn't be wasted. There might be a place for you in the new order of things if you want it."

"A place? What kind of place? And why me?" Hart was confused. One minute this woman was threatening her with a gun; the next, she was offering her a place in the new America. Who was Valentin, anyhow?

"You understand solar technology. And engines. And you seem to have no . . . unfortunate political affiliations."

145

Astonished, Hart was speechless for a moment. Things were happening too fast. "I need to think about all this," Hart said weakly.

"Of course," Valentin said. She glanced at Hart, and just for an instant Hart thought she saw an echo of the feral smile she had seen on the flatbed. But when Hart blinked, it was gone.

"Why don't you call up the computer's topographic maps and find us a high point?" Valentin said. "We're going to use the radio, and I need a line of sight for the aerial. Pick something just beyond the pass."

Hart asked the computer for AERIAL LOCATE, and watched as the maps flipped by.

"Hang on," Valentin said. She made a quick adjustment Hart couldn't see and then, with a surge of power, the SunRaycer jumped into the air.

"We're . . . it *flies!*" Hart exclaimed.

"Well, it can make short hops," Valentin explained. "To clear obstacles."

"I didn't think that was possible," Hart said. "In fact, I don't remember anything like the SunRaycer from the days before BioStrike. Solar-powered automobiles were only a dream."

"The SunRaycer is a recent development," Valentin told her. "It has an enormous array of storage batteries under the floor. Thanks to a new alloy developed on my country's space station, and a new miniaturized design, we can store one hundred times the power we could ten years ago."

"Really?" Hart asked, excited. "But how did you solve the problem of collecting the energy? I remember the solar collectors I used. They were only

146

about fifteen percent efficient, and they were state-of-the-art."

"Well, these are different. They're energy panels and they're one hundred percent efficient," Valentin said. "You see, we don't collect the energy here on earth."

"What?"

Valentin chuckled. "No. We collect it in space. Enormous mirrors direct the solar energy to the space station where it's turned into microwaves and beamed to the SunRaycer's energy panels." She patted the car's dash. "So even though this vehicle uses the sun's power, it isn't directly solar powered. For instance, if the sun goes behind a cloud, we're still in business."

"Fascinating."

Valentin gave Hart a conspiratorial grin. "We're going to get along well, you and I. I think we're two of a kind."

Hart smiled back politely, but as the ground receded beneath her, she had a terrible moment of panic. She stole a look at Valentin — face bathed in the otherworldly green glow of the instrument panel — and her heart thumped with fear. Stop it, she told herself sternly. Just stop it. Everything will be all right.

CHAPTER 8

The bravest are surely those who have the clearest vision of what is before them, glory and danger alike, and yet notwithstanding go out to meet it.

Aristophanes,
History of the Peloponnesian War

Sandoval floated, light and insubstantial as gossamer, far above the wreck of the train. Whatever body she had had, she had left behind and now her spirit soared free. But she was not completely free —

she knew that. A duty had been laid on her. Where the gods live, some bargain had been made. Something had been given her, or returned to her, and in exchange she was to perform some task. So she waited in midair, her spirit hovering like a kestrel.

Light flickered below her in the forest, and she fell, drawn to it like a moth. And what she fell into was a meadow. A green alpine meadow. Grasses grew knee-high, reaching from the forest's edge down to the shore of a pocket-sized lake. In the verge where trees and grass met, wild things prowled. She saw their eyes reflecting moonlight. Stars fallen from the sky were scattered across the damp ground — the turquoise lamps of glowworms shining from the edges of rocks, clumps of grass. At the lake's far end, a little waterfall poured over a cliff and emptied into a pool. Two small bats, fluttering like butterflies, dipped down to skim mouthfuls of water from the pool. In the forest behind her a screech owl whistled, a soft, hollow sound repeated slowly, ending in a tremulous trill. And with her preternatural sight, she saw starlight sparkling like crushed diamonds in the eyes of a spider.

This was what she had been brought here to see, this vision. She knew it. So she looked. And looked again, trying to find meaning. Against the sky, backlit by the stars, the jagged teeth of the mountains were an eloquent calligraphy. But they did not speak to her. Deaf to them, she knew some final secret had been withheld.

"Wait," she cried. "Tell me what you want me to know!" The spell shattered as she spoke, and suddenly she felt herself falling. Wind whistled in her ears as the meadow rushed up to meet her, and the lights went out one by one like snuffed candles. Gravity claimed her, and she fell to earth, descending through the dark into her body.

*****

Sandoval awakened, certain that her scalp had been peeled off and refitted wrong side out with all the nerves exposed. And inside, deep within her cranium, a booming persisted, as if her head were a hollow vessel into which people were shouting. What had happened, she wondered, opening her eyes. Her mind took in three things at once: that she was lying in one of the MedCenter vans, that Corporal Lujan was sleeping, head on her arms, in a chair beside her bed, and that outside it was bright daylight.

For a moment she was disoriented, and she clutched the sides of her cot, feeling nauseated and dizzy. A fragment of a dream floated through her mind like a wisp of smoke, and she recalled for one fleeting moment a spider's diamond eyes. And then the dream was gone, leaving an echo of lost beauty like a chord of unbearably lovely music. She drew a ragged breath and sat up.

"Captain!" Lujan said, springing out of her chair.

Sandoval groaned, and raised both hands to cradle her throbbing head.

The van door opened and Dr. Ashe stuck her head inside. "So, you're awake," she said gruffly.

"I seem to be," Sandoval said, her tongue thick. "What in hell happened to me?"

"You don't remember?" Lujan asked, concerned.

Sandoval looked at the young corporal. Somewhere

150

Lujan had discarded her black long-sleeved shirt. She now wore only her gray singlet, and her black pants. Her weapons belt, Sandoval noted, was nowhere in sight. "You're out of uniform, Corporal," she said.

"I, er, yes I am, Captain," Lujan admitted. "But someone needed my shirt."

"Hmmph," Sandoval said, trying furiously to remember. What *had* happened to her? She recalled standing in the middle of the railway car among the Gaians, then. . . . She closed her eyes. She remembered now. The train had been derailed. She had been tossed about the car like a leaf in a gale, tangled with dozens of other women, finally coming to rest in a heap of bodies. She had lost consciousness then, and had only regained it when Lujan and Hart were dragging her up the hillside.

"I remember," Sandoval told Lujan. "Report, Corporal."

Lujan took a deep breath. "The train is a complete wreck. The engine hit a tree on the tracks — Rincon thinks it was a trap — and most of the cars jumped the rails. All except this one are scattered down the side of the ravine. Two went over the edge."

"Casualties?" Sandoval asked, prepared for the worst.

"Twelve troopers lost. Four others wounded — broken bones and so on. Only three of us — well, four now — escaped without injury."

"What about the Gaians?"

"That car suffered the worst. Half of it slid over the cliff when Hart and I were down there. The other half went over shortly after."

Sandoval was appalled. "Then none of the women are left alive?"

Lujan shook her head. "Hart and I pulled five of them out and dragged them a little ways up the hill."

"My God," Sandoval said.

"Some of the Arizona medteam personnel survived," Lujan offered. "Dr. Ashe and one of the medtechs were back here on the vehicles flatbed when the crash happened. Ashe's assistant didn't make it, though — the woman named Medina."

Sandoval stood up shakily, her hand on Lujan's shoulder. Apart from her throbbing head, everything seemed intact. "Tell me who can walk out of here," she said.

"Me, you, Estefan, and Rincon for sure. Probably Lau and Flores. Ashe and her medtech Montalvo. And a couple of Gaians — Onava, Irena, and a woman named Rowan. Maybe eleven of us. That's it."

"Valentin," Sandoval said, suddenly remembering. "What about Valentin? And Hart?"

"Well," Lujan said, plainly puzzled. "That's an odd thing. They're nowhere around. Ashe says she saw Valentin head off into the woods with Hart."

"With Hart?" Sandoval asked, her mind woolly. What would Valentin want with Hart? Then she had it. "The SunRaycer!" she exclaimed. "Damn it to hell. Where's Dr. Ashe?"

"Are you —"

"Don't worry. I'm all right." She patted the other woman on the arm and stood alone, proving it. "I'm fine." Opening the van door, she winced as a flood of bright sunlight poured in.

"I moved all the vehicles off the flatbed and parked them over there in the woods," Lujan

152

explained. "Ashe wanted the space for the wounded. And I've rounded up all the usable supplies — food, water, weapons, extra clothes, and so on — and piled them there by the other van."

Sandoval looked back over her shoulder at the young woman and smiled. "So, Corporal, you were in command last night. What do you think of the position?"

Lujan grimaced. "I'm glad you're all right, Ma'am. I didn't much like it."

"Well, it seems as though you made the right decisions. But there's something I have to find out. Take me to Dr. Ashe."

* * * * *

"Damn!" Ashe swore. "The box was right here. I wouldn't have moved it. We were awfully busy last night, though. I suppose in the confusion, anyone could have come in here and taken the vaccine. Although the warning on the outside of the container should have been enough to scare anyone off."

"What did it say?" Sandoval asked.

Ashe grimaced. "RD Vaccine Prototype. Warning: Contains Live Virus. Extremely Dangerous."

Sandoval shook her head. "It wouldn't have deterred Lieutenant Valentin."

"But why steal the vaccine?" Ashe asked. "For God's sake, I was supposed to *give* it to her. I can't imagine what she could do with it outside a research facility."

Sandoval looked at Ashe. "What do you mean?"

"Well, the vaccine can't be used as it is. For one

thing, it's been lyophilized — freeze-dried. It has to be reconstituted. And you can't just add water and shake. You have to add sterile physiological saline, and in the right proportion, too." She shook her head. "It's all but useless unless it's delivered into the hands of someone who knows what she's doing."

Sandoval thought for a moment. She knew of no medical research facility still operational in Los Angeles. The major hospitals were now warehouses for the transfusion of Stage One Positives — those lucky enough to have been categorized as "essential personnel" by BioStrike Central. So what *did* Valentin intend to do with the vaccine?

"Why did she take Hart along with her?" Ashe asked. "You don't suppose —" She let the question hang in the air.

"No!" Lujan said emphatically. "Hart didn't steal the vaccine for her."

Sandoval raised an eyebrow at Lujan's impassioned outburst. "You seem awfully sure of that, Corporal."

"I am," Lujan said. "She risked her life last night. She's no thief."

Sandoval shrugged. "She might be, Lujan. Whether she helped you or not, she has no particular reason to like the BioStrike Forces. After all, we kidnapped her. We shot her. We took her blood. We threw her into that railway car."

Lujan was silent for a moment. "Then why would she have helped Valentin? She's a member of the BioStrike Forces, too."

"It wouldn't be too difficult to tell Hart a fairy tale," Ashe said wearily. "Solar Tech Hart desperately wants something to believe in. Something bigger than herself. Something that makes more sense than a struggle for survival. Valentin may have convinced her that there is such a thing. Or she may have put a gun to her head and convinced her that way."

Sandoval shook her head. "Well, whether Hart was forced or went willingly, whether she stole the vaccine or is entirely innocent of its presence, she's in for a big surprise."

"Oh?" Ashe asked. "What?"

"Lieutenant Valentin can hardly take her to whatever BioStrike outpost she's making for," Sandoval pointed out. "Hart is the property of the Republic of California — the only way she should arrive is under guard in a boxcar, not riding in style in the SunRaycer. Valentin would be accused of appropriating military property for her own use." She shook her head. "No, I imagine that once Hart has served her purpose Valentin will simply dispose of her.

Ashe sat down heavily. "Do you mean Valentin will kill her?"

"Yes," Sandoval said. "I do."

* * * * *

As soon as Sandoval saw the wounded, she knew she had to do something drastic. Although her troopers presented cheerful faces, Sandoval could tell they were in pain. And those with broken bones needed rest. Like wounded animals, they needed to crawl away into their dens and heal.

She sat on the ground with the other able-bodied women, eating the meal that Onava and her women had been able to concoct.

155

"Do you think the tree across the tracks was a trap?" Lujan asked Sandoval.

Sandoval considered this, examining her grain cereal with little appetite. "It could be," she answered. "If it is, the trapper will soon be along to check his snare, don't you think?"

Lujan looked apprehensively into the forest. "That's what Rincon thought. She should be back soon. I sent her and Estefan ahead to reconnoiter."

Sandoval smiled. Precisely what she would have done. "You've done well, Lujan," she said.

The young woman flushed with pleasure.

"Tell me," Sandoval asked, genuinely interested, "if you were still in command, what would you do?"

Lujan answered shyly, "While you were unconscious, I thought about that a lot." She hurried to explain, "Just in case I had to take command, you understand."

"Go on," Sandoval encouraged her.

"Well," Lujan said, "depending on what Rincon and Estefan find up ahead, I'd move the wounded to the first suitable place — someplace where we could build shelters, and where there was firewood and water. Then I'd send a party after that damned Valentin."

"Oh?" Sandoval asked. "I would think you'd be better off radioing ahead to the nearest BioStrike outpost for medical supplies and food, then sending a party. Why waste your energy chasing Valentin?"

Lujan looked at Sandoval in consternation. "But . . ." she trailed off. "God, you don't know. I didn't tell you."

"Tell me what?" Sandoval demanded.

156

Lujan scowled. "Valentin took our radio with her. In the SunRaycer."

"Damn it to hell!" Sandoval shouted.

"Sorry," Lujan said quietly.

"It's all right," Sandoval said, standing up. "It's certainly not your fault. If it's anyone's, it's mine for not seeing through her earlier." She handed Lujan her empty bowl. "My compliments to chef Onava." Shading her eyes, she looked around at the ruin of her BioStrike Unit. More deaths on her conscience. More broken bodies. Maybe Valentin had been right, she thought sadly. Maybe she was no longer fit to command.

"Look," said Lujan, pointing up the tracks. "Rincon and Estefan."

"Good," Sandoval said, abruptly coming to a decision. "See that they get something to eat, then have them report to me in half an hour in that little clearing over there. You come, too, and bring me an inventory of our supplies. And tell Ashe and Montalvo to come. I want Ashe to make a similar inventory. And we'd better have Onava present. Ask her to bring one of her women with her. Someone responsible." She looked hard at Lujan. "If you had to take charge of what's left of this unit, who would you choose for a second-in-command?"

Lujan answered without hesitation. "Private Rincon. She's tough-minded, sensible, and smart. And she's got guts."

Sandoval smiled. "Thank you, Corporal. I'll see you in half an hour."

* * * * *

157

Sandoval sat on a fallen log in the clearing, waiting for the others to join her. She felt a profound depression, but also an enormous anger. This mission had been ill-fated right from the start. She had lost several of her troopers in that raid on the Nevada donor camp three weeks ago, and now twelve more as the result of this train wreck. As well, four were too badly hurt to walk. She shook her head.

How would she ever resolve this mess? She closed her eyes. To carry out her original orders, she would have to deliver Ashe and the remnants of the Gaians to BioStrike Central in Los Angeles. That was now impossible, as there was no transportation available.

Another option was to deliver Ashe and the Gaians to the nearest BioStrike outpost. That was a little more feasible. She recalled from her study of the map that the nearest outpost was about two hundred miles northwest of them. Difficult, but not impossible. But also, not a project for the present time.

The limiting factor in both these plans was, of course, transportation. Well, that problem could be solved. Once she had recovered the radio from Valentin, she could send ahead for help, and have BioStrike Central dispatch vehicles. That would be simple enough. And in the time it would take her to catch up with Valentin, the women could be resting. Recovering their strength. After all, they were going to be absolutely useless as donors if they were ill. She looked over at the pitiful group of Gaians. Only six remained.

And Ashe? Could she now hand over Ashe to BioStrike Central, knowing the trouble that the outspoken, irascible physician would likely cause for herself?

And what about her troopers? The sooner she got them safely back to a BioStrike outpost, the sooner they could be transferred to other units. That the Sixth was finished, she now had no doubt.

And what about you, she asked herself? What fate awaits you?

She looked back over her shoulder. Two of the Gaian women were standing with two of her troopers — Lau and Flores — and the four women were laughing together. As Sandoval watched, Lau took off her heavy black shirt and gave it to one of the Gaians to put on. The woman reached into a pocket of her skirt, and unfolded a bright yellow bandana. Reaching up shyly, for Lau was much taller, she tied the bandana around Lau's forehead. Her hands lingered a moment longer than necessary in Lau's hair, and Sandoval realized suddenly that something was happening here over which neither she nor BioStrike Central had any control.

She looked around, and it was as if she had just been granted sight. Ashe sat on a rock, talking with one of the Gaians; Lujan and Onava were carrying on an animated conversation. It was an ordinary, peaceful scene.

And suddenly she knew why she was hesitating. Why she didn't want to chase Valentin, get the radio, send for help, and allow the BioStrike machine to chew her up again. She was tired. She wanted peace.

Frightened, she closed her eyes. *What's happening to me,* she thought desperately. If she truly believed in her cause, she would follow her orders and march Ashe and the Gaians to Los Angeles. Wiser heads than hers had devised these orders — who was she to question them? But I do question them, she thought.

159

Touching the back of her head gingerly, she was mindful of her own mortality. She thought of the train wreck, and of the women who had been in the car with her. Why, of all of them, had she, Onava, and the madwoman been spared? She thought of Lujan and Hart dragging her up the hillside, of Lujan's tale of how she and Hart had saved each others' lives. Was there a pattern at work here, a design she was unable to see?

The dead don't need me, she told herself. Perhaps the living do. Perhaps I can give them a new chance, a chance to be safe. She recalled the Gaian tying the yellow bandana around Lau's head, and how Lau had looked at her. Perhaps that's why I was spared, she thought. She looked back at the few women left standing, and a wave of fierce protectiveness washed over her, more powerful than any she had felt for her troopers alone.

I can do this, she thought excitedly. I can arrange for all of us to be lost. An unfortunate accident. Massive casualties. But I need that damned radio. And I need to stop Valentin.

* * * * *

"Thank you for taking time from your various tasks," she told the women seated around her — Ashe and a small dark-haired medtech named Montalvo, Rincon and Estefan, Onava and a shrewd-faced woman named Rowan, and Lujan and Lau. "I asked you here because you each represent a different interest group. And I need your help."

Ashe crossed her arms and raised one eyebrow but

160

said nothing. Rincon and Estefan exchanged quick glances.

"We'll all be leaving here soon," she told them. "Corporal Lujan and I have an errand to perform a little farther up the tracks. In our absence, Private Rincon will be in command of the Sixth." She looked meaningfully at Onava and Ashe. "I'm asking you to see to it that your women cooperate with Rincon."

"Why should we?" Rowan asked. A small redhead in dirty khaki pants and a well-worn blue shirt, she seemed to be perpetually calculating. "You've brought us nothing but grief."

Sandoval looked at her and nodded. "That's true. I have. But when I return — with our stolen radio, with medical supplies, and with additional transportation — I intend to do something to help you."

"What?" Onava asked, her face lined with pain. Her forehead bore a large, dark bruise, and she carried her left arm in a sling made from strips of her skirt. Mementos of the train crash. "What can you possibly do to help us?"

"I can set you free," Sandoval told them. "Turn you loose. You can go wherever you choose. I'll see to it that my troopers give you whatever transport we can spare. You can go wherever you like. And if you need it, we'll give you help to get there."

Onava said nothing, but Sandoval sensed she was thinking about her offer very carefully.

"You said when you return. Why do we have to wait? Why not let us go now?"

"Because right now we all need each other," Sandoval said. "None of us is strong enough to go anywhere alone. We need Ashe's medical expertise, your knowledge of edible and medicinal plants, and my troopers' weapons and skills. We need to form an alliance. And I need to know that I can trust all of you to keep your parts of the bargain."

"Tell us again what you're offering," Onava asked.

"To help you go home. Or wherever else you choose."

"What about us?" Ashe asked quietly. "Does that apply to us, too? We can't go back to Tucson, you know."

"It applies to you," Sandoval told her, smiling wryly. "You'll think of someplace you want to go, Doctor. I'm sure of it."

Ashe looked at the ground, then back up at Sandoval. "What if you don't come back?"

"Then Private Rincon will honor my part of the bargain." She looked over at Rincon.

"If the Captain doesn't return, I'll do whatever I reasonably can to keep the bargain," Rincon said formally, standing up and smoothing the creases out of her black shirt and pants. She stood tall and straight as she answered Ashe, brown eyes earnest.

"All right," Onava said.

Ashe nodded. "I agree."

Sandoval let out the breath she had been holding. "Fine. That leaves us only one more issue to discuss." She looked around. "The Red Death."

"I had almost forgotten about it," Ashe said. "We have so many other afflictions."

"We've had so much blood spilled in the last little while that it would be a miracle if the Stage Ones haven't infected others," Sandoval said. She looked at

Ashe. "Do we have sufficient testing equipment left? And materials?"

Ashe nodded. "Yes. For a few more testing sessions, anyhow."

Onava broke in. "And what will you do with those who are found to be positive?"

Sandoval ran a hand through her hair. "I haven't the faintest idea. You'll have to sort that out."

Onava looked at Ashe. "Doctor? What do you propose?"

"There are only so many choices," Ashe told her.

"And what are they?"

"Euthanize them, ostracize them, or transfuse them," Ashe said brutally.

Onava shook her head firmly. "Those are unacceptable. We would prefer to let Gaia have her way with us."

"That's very attractive philosophically," Sandoval observed, "but hardly practical."

"Why not?" Rowan demanded.

"Because if any of you Gaians now have the virus, you'll surely pass it to those of us who don't. We'll be working too closely together to escape it. No, we're all in this together. I propose that we do as Dr. Ashe advises. This is her field of expertise, after all."

Onava looked at Sandoval in stony silence. "What *does* Dr. Ashe advise?" she asked at length.

"Depending on the numbers of Stage Ones, we can transfuse," Ashe said. "Not with the blood we had in the cooler — those containers were smashed. We can use the RD negatives as donors. But that's just a holding action."

Sandoval scowled. "I know. Sooner or later the Stage Ones will turn into Stage Twos. Then what?

And how do we ensure that the Stage Ones keep the virus to themselves?" She suddenly thought of Lau and the woman with the yellow bandana.

"We can't do a thing, really, for the Stage Ones," Ashe said. "But we can sure as hell do something for the others. The RD negatives."

Sandoval looked at Ashe curiously. "Oh? What?"

"The vaccine."

"But you told me that the vaccine would be useless," Sandoval reminded her. What was Ashe talking about?

"To Valentin. Or to anyone without a smattering of medical research experience. Or proper facilities. Hell, I developed the bloody thing," she said. "I do know how to reconstitute it. And if we can hang onto the MedCenter vans, I'll have the facilities."

"But you said it's experimental," Sandoval objected, not wanting to hope.

"Yes it is. And some of the people died who tested it. But think of the thousands who have died from the Red Death."

Sandoval felt Ashe looking at her. The doctor stood, hands on her hips, head cocked to one side, appraising Sandoval. *Here's your chance,* she seemed to be saying. *Do something useful.* Sandoval smiled ruefully at her and stood up. There was, it seemed, very little time to waste.

"Private Rincon tells me that she and Estefan found an encampment of what seems to be blood sellers about three miles down the tracks, in an abandoned town. It was probably they who set the trap. Sooner or later they'll come looking. I don't want them to find you here. You'll have to bury the dead quickly and move the wounded to a safer place.

Estefan says she found a little box canyon back down the tracks half a mile or so. There's water and firewood."

Ashe and Onava looked around as if sensing the urgency. "What about the vehicles?" Ashe asked. "The MedCenter vans?"

"They can be driven down the tracks and into the canyon," Rincon said. "It will be rough on the wounded, but it's the fastest way of getting them there. The OLVs can be pressed into service, too."

Sandoval was relieved when Onava spoke up, offering help. "We'll show you how to cover your tracks," she said. "And how to block off the canyon from view."

"Thank you," Rincon said. She turned to Sandoval. "Captain, there will only be a few of us troopers, but I think we should have round-the-clock sentries. We don't want to be surprised."

"Agreed," Sandoval said. She looked at the three women: Ashe, Onava, and Rincon. An unlikely triad. Yet stranger alliances had been made. Well, it would have to do.

"Corporal," she said to Lujan, "I suggest you assemble some supplies for us. I'll meet you at the flatbed."

"Thank you," she said to the women. "Lujan and I will be back as soon as we can manage it."

* * * * *

Sandoval knelt with Lujan, portioning out the supplies they would need.

"It's the water that weighs so much," Lujan said. "And it's impossible to know how much to take."

"Whatever we can carry," Sandoval said. "The load will only get lighter as we go along."

"Do you think we'll catch them?" Lujan asked.

"I'm sure of it."

"How can you be sure?"

"Lieutenant Valentin is a great believer in maps," Sandoval said. "But they don't tell the whole story. A fire swept through that pass last year. There are trees down all over the road. Nothing except maybe the OLVs could get through."

"Then we *will* catch them!"

"Oh, we'll catch them," Sandoval said. "After that —"

"Captain," a voice called from behind her. "A word if you please."

Sandoval turned. Ashe stood there, hands in the pockets of her coveralls. "I, that is, we . . ." She trailed off and fixed Lujan with an eloquent look.

"I think I'll go and siphon off some gas for the OLV," Lujan said tactfully.

"Something on your mind, Doctor?" Sandoval inquired, shouldering her pack. She picked up her helmet, considered it, then added it to the pile of supplies. Better take it, she thought.

Ashe cleared her throat. "I need a gun."

"A gun?" Sandoval repeated. "What for?" Sandoval saw how hard this was for the other woman to say.

"For the Stage Twos," Ashe told Sandoval, her voice choked. "My drug cabinet suffered in the crash. I have none of the drugs I would normally use to alleviate pain. Or for euthanasia. And with Stage Two, it's just a question of time anyhow. Isn't it?"

Sandoval reached down and unclipped her holster

166

from her belt. "Here," she said, handing the holstered gun to Ashe. "This is an old-fashioned relic. A Colt .45 U.S. Army Officer's model. It's an automatic." She counted out a dozen bullets from her weapons belt and handed them to Ashe. "You do know how to fire this, I presume?"

Ashe nodded.

"I've had that gun for nineteen years," Sandoval said. "It's saved my life more times than I can count."

"Thank you," Ashe said. She put the gun and the shells in one of the voluminous pockets of her coveralls. She patted the pocket closed, then looked at Sandoval. With a quick spasm of pity Sandoval took in the lines of fatigue on the doctor's face, the dirt and bloodstains on her coveralls. And something else. Something that Ashe was clearly trying to hide. Fear.

Ashe held a hand out to Sandoval. "Good luck," she said, her voice husky. "And come back. They — we — need you."

Sandoval took Ashe's hand in both of hers. Surprised and deeply moved, she was unable to trust her voice for a moment. "I'll be back," she told Ashe when she was able to speak. "You can count on it."

CHAPTER 9

O villain, villain, smiling damned villain!
My tables — meet it is I set it down,
That one may smile, and smile, and be a villain . . .
William Shakespeare, *Hamlet*

"Damn!" Valentin swore, looking at the log-choked road. "There must have been a fire. Why in hell didn't those troopers bring their maps up to date?" She checked the gauge on the instrument panel. "I'd exhaust the storage batteries jumping this mess. Hart, where are we?"

Hart looked at the glowing dot on the computer's screen, read off the coordinates, and referred to the paper map she held in her hands. "Here," she said. "Just south of Oak Creek." She peered more closely at the map. "There's a little town here. Or at least there was. It's called Oak Creek, too. On this map it has a red star beside it. Does that mean anything?"

Valentin shrugged. "I don't know. Let's get this thing off the road and get the radio set up. I want to do something before we go on into Oak Creek."

Valentin pulled the SunRaycer off the road, cursing in a language Hart didn't understand. Opening the SunRaycer's bubble roof, she handed Hart a stiff length of copper wire.

"Embarrassingly antiquated," she said critically. "But I suppose we should be grateful that the BioStrike Forces have *any* communications equipment at all." Then she pointed to a nearby pine. "Up you go. Try and position the antenna so it clears the top of that tree. Give me ten minutes or so after you get set up. Then dismantle everything and come on down."

Hart looked up at the tree Valentin had indicated. It seemed climbable. "Are you signaling BioStrike Central?" Hart asked.

Valentin laughed. "No, Hart. And in fact I won't be signaling at all — I'll be listening."

"Oh? To what?"

"To the sounds of Sanctuary, my young friend."

Hart almost dropped the antenna. "Sanctuary? So it *is* real!"

"Of course it's real," Valentin said testily. "A group of addle-brained women fleeing their responsibilities."

169

"But I thought the BioStrike Forces wouldn't be interested in Sanctuary," Hart said.

"I assure you, Hart," Valentin said grimly, "I'm very interested in Sanctuary. And so are my superiors. Sanctuary's leaders are not only foolish dreamers, they're dangerous reactionaries. They infect others with false hope — dreams of a new world." She laughed in derision. "No, they have to be found and eradicated. Ruthlessly. When we take over —" She looked at Hart, seemed to think better of what she was about to say, and turned away.

Hart began to climb.

* * * * *

Hart affixed the wire to the tallest point of the pine she could reach, then settled back to wait. The wind ruffled her hair, and she looked back down the road, thinking of the women at the train. She still felt somewhat guilty about leaving them, but quickly reminded herself that Valentin *had* spoken to Dr. Ashe. And as Valentin had pointed out, Dr. Ashe didn't need her; Valentin did. Still, Hart thought resentfully, she didn't have to use her pistol to make the point.

A gust of wind shook the tree, threatening to dislodge the antenna, and Hart reached up, tightening the cord with which she had tied the wire to the branch. Why are you doing this, she asked herself as she pulled the cord tighter. Valentin doesn't feel the same way you do about Sanctuary. You heard her — she thinks the women who fled there are dangerous, a threat to others. She'd like nothing better than to

170

locate them, round them all up, and march them to BioStrike Central. So why are you helping her?

"Hart!" Valentin called from down below. "I can't get anything. Come on down."

Relieved, Hart unhooked the aerial and dropped it to the ground. The women of Sanctuary were safe for another little while. But if Valentin persisted, Hart was sure that the Lieutenant would locate them. In fact, Hart was sure that Valentin could do anything she chose. The woman seemed . . . superhuman. Hart thought of Valentin's wintry blue eyes and swallowed a little in fear. It wasn't just Valentin's pistol that made Hart so acquiescent, she admitted, feeling ashamed. It was Valentin herself. She was afraid of Valentin in a way she had never been afraid of Sandoval. Valentin seemed to burn with a cold, interior flame — the flame of fanaticism. Hart had seen fanatics before — in the months following BioStrike — and had observed how associating with them brought only grief. Fanatics required sacrifices. But there was something else, too, something she had only now acknowledged. Something more shameful than cowardice. She recalled Valentin's clasp on her knee, Valentin's hand brushing her cheek, Valentin's smile as she complimented some act of cleverness on Hart's part. Hart closed her eyes. Was she a child to need Valentin's praise so? Or was it something else she needed from Valentin? Angry now, she coiled the excess wire into a bundle and threw it to the ground. Then, taking less care than she should have, she shimmied down the scaly tower of the pine tree.

* * * * *

171

Valentin was packing up the radio when Hart reached the ground. Fat drops of rain had already begun to splat on the ground, and the air had grown noticeably colder. Shivering, Hart handed the antenna and coil of wire to the other woman, who packed everything away into a watertight case. Valentin lifted the roof of the SunRaycer, and Hart saw her reposition a white styrofoam box in the small cargo hold of the SunRaycer. Black, stenciled lettering said TUCSON MEDCENTER — ASHE on one side, and Hart suddenly realized what it was. The vaccine! But why had Valentin brought it with them? Weren't they going to contact BioStrike Central for help for the beleaguered train? Hart had thought that BioStrike Central would send troops for the wounded and the vaccine. At least that was what Valentin had led her to believe.

"Did you hear anything?" Hart asked, hoping she hadn't.

Valentin shrugged. "The reception was poor. It must be the storm."

"Do you think Sanctuary's close by?" Hart wondered, trying to sound casual.

"No. It's on the north coast somewhere," Valentin said, preoccupied.

Hart tried her best to hide the elation she felt. She had just learned more about Sanctuary in thirty seconds from Valentin than she had in two years of listening to radio transmissions.

Valentin put on her helmet, buckled on her weapons belt, and motioned Hart to join her. She handed her a backpack, and Hart shrugged into it.

"We'll leave the SunRaycer here and walk into Oak Creek," Valentin said. "Why huddle here in the

172

car when we can get indoors? Maybe build a fire. Then, once we get back here, I need to see about getting re-charged from our satellite when it passes overhead. You'll be interested in the procedure."

"Do you think it's safe in Oak Creek?" Hart asked. "Some of these little towns are, well, blood-seller camps."

Valentin flipped her visor down with a *snick* of finality. "I'm a BioStrike officer. No one would dare interfere with me. Really, Hart. You need to display more self-confidence if you're going to be a member of the new order."

Hart said nothing. She wasn't at all sure that she wanted membership in Valentin's club. But she decided that the wisest course of action was to remain mute.

* * * * *

From the road leading into town, Hart could see that Oak Creek was nothing more than a collection of ramshackle cabins beside a fast-flowing stream. But the cabins were far from deserted. Smoke rose from several chimneys, horses were tied to makeshift hitching posts, and a jeep sat in the road, its left front wheel missing.

"Civilization," Valentin commented, as the rain began in earnest. "Pick a cabin, Hart."

Hart pointed to a nearby cabin, one which seemed in good repair. Valentin led the way. To Hart's amazement, she simply marched up onto the porch and pounded on the door.

"Open up!" she called. "This is Lieutenant Valentin of the Sixth BioStrike Unit."

173

The door was opened a crack. "A BioStrike trooper!" a surprised male voice exclaimed. "So the brat was right. He did sell us to the blackshirts. What did you give him for us, you devil? How much are human lives worth?"

Valentin put the toe of her boot in the partly open doorway. "Stop babbling," she told the man in disgust. "We need shelter and a fire. I am ordering you to provide it. Under the BioStrike Edicts, to refuse is treason." Appalled, Hart watched as Valentin drew her pistol.

The door swung open. "Come in," a thin, bearded man said grudgingly. He was dressed in a well-mended pair of gray trousers and a frayed, red-checkered flannel shirt.

Valentin pushed past him, looked around in disapproval, and finally took an overstuffed chair by the fire. Hart followed the bearded man's eyes — a knife, some strips of leather, and a ceramic mug and plate sat on the floor by the chair. Obviously the man had been at work, Hart thought. They had interrupted his meal, and now Valentin had taken his chair.

"Sit down," Valentin told him. "Over there on the hearth will do nicely."

His dislike barely disguised, the man sat down.

"Tell me about Oak Creek," Valentin said. "What goes on here?"

The man glared at her. "Don't you know? Didn't the little merchant tell you when he betrayed us?" He scratched his beard. "We should never have taken pity on those children."

Valentin regarded him coolly. "Stop raving and answer my question."

The man chewed at a hangnail. "What does it matter — we're dead people now. There were so few of us anyway," he said. "We used to farm a little. Two of the men hunted. I fished sometimes. Mostly we just tried to get by." He gestured to the bookshelves that lined his walls. "We were trying to . . . preserve things. Books. Videotapes." His eyes filled with tears. "Knowledge of the past. Memories."

Valentin shook her head, clearly disgusted. "What about the Red Death?"

"We didn't have it. Everyone who did was dead long ago." He eyed her meaningfully. "That's why we made it a rule never to have anything to do with strangers. We knew we were clean. We wanted to stay that way." He shook his head sorrowfully. "But the children . . . they were so pitiful. So needy."

"What children?" Hart felt compelled to ask. "Are they —"

Valentin raised a hand and interrupted her in mid-sentence. Intimidated, Hart fell silent.

Valentin stretched her feet out closer to the fire. Thunder rumbled outside, and with an ear-splitting crash, the storm hit. Hart could hardly hear Valentin's next question for the roar of the rain. "How many of you are left here in Oak Creek?" Valentin asked.

"Four," the man said.

Valentin smiled. "Three, now," she told him. Raising her pistol, she shot him in the chest. Thrown back against the fireplace, he remained sitting for a moment, eyes open in incredulity. Then he slumped to the floor.

Hart stood rooted to the spot, unable to move. "No!" she cried out, looking at Valentin in horror.

175

"You didn't have to do that!" Hart was trembling so badly she thought her knees would buckle. This isn't real, she told herself. It's not happening. No one behaves like this.

"Oh?" Valentin asked. "Didn't I? The man was clearly uncooperative. He might have been a threat later." She picked up the man's mug and sniffed its contents. "Coffee," she commented. "The real thing." When Hart said nothing, she looked over at her. "Come here my squeamish young friend."

Hart came to stand beside Valentin's chair. Valentin reached up and took Hart's hand. "As cold as ice," she commented. "Go on into the kitchen and find that coffee. Make us both some. I'll put more wood on the fire."

Hart looked over at the man's body and swallowed.

Valentin laughed softly. "Don't worry about him," she told Hart. "He's dead. He can't bother us. Now go do what I told you to. And look around in there to see what you can find to eat. We'll have a good meal, courtesy of our friend here, wait out the storm, and then move on." She squeezed Hart's hand encouragingly, then let it go. "We're going to have to toughen you up somehow."

Hart walked like an automaton to the kitchen. This is all a dream, she told herself. Or a nightmare. Opening a cupboard, she looked at the meager store of supplies — sugar, salt, pepper, flour, cornmeal. Each glass jar had been carefully labeled, and the supplies had been arranged in order of size. She opened another cupboard. Plates and cups in several different patterns of china were stacked there, but everything was clean. In a pantry beside the stove she found a treasure trove. Seven unopened cans of Maxwell House coffee, Hershey's chocolate bars in a huge glass jar, and a case of Jameson's Scotch. This man had been a very farsighted individual. On the woodstove, a pot of coffee simmered. She reached for the pot, and that was when it all hit her.

Valentin had killed that man. Killed him for no reason at all. Killed him as casually as she, Hart, would have stepped on a spider. Her hands began to shake so badly she knew she didn't dare pick up the pot. She leaned against the sink, looking out through the little window at the rain, feeling sick.

"What's taking you so long?" Valentin called.

"I'm coming," Hart answered. "I'm just finding things." What am I going to do, she asked herself in desperation. I can't go anywhere with this killer. She only wants me with her because I can fix things. And when I'm no longer useful to her . . . Hart felt an icy chill on the back of her neck, realizing suddenly that Valentin could dispose of her as easily as she had killed that man in the living room. And did she really plan to plead Hart's case with BioStrike Central? Hart doubted it. Why should she? A terrible anger began to grow in her, and with it, a terrible resolve.

She thought with a pang of the last time she had seen Sandoval, stumbling like a drunk into the MedCenter van. For no good reason, she had been suddenly, absolutely certain that the Captain was going to wake up, look at the wreckage around her, and relent, releasing them all. She had been sure of that. Instead, Sandoval had died. And Ashe, Medina, and the Gaians were still prisoners of the BioStrike forces, and still doomed.

Then, an idea began to grow in her mind, something so audacious, so daring that it took her breath away. She closed her eyes, and suddenly the plan was there, fully formed. It would demand cool-headedness. Daring. And if it failed, she would forfeit everything. Including her life. Well, what of it? She had no future here, trapped with Valentin. Perhaps the time had come to take some risks. She hadn't been much good to Ashe so far, had she? With a little luck, she would change all that.

Selecting a mug from the cupboard, she poured Valentin's coffee. She would have to dissemble. She didn't dare let Valentin know her true feelings. She needed to allay the other woman's suspicions — if indeed she had any — until she had learned everything she needed to know. Hoping her horror and revulsion didn't show, she walked, coffee mug in hand, back into the living room.

Valentin took the coffee, eyeing her. "You don't approve of what I did," she said neutrally, her light eyes expressionless.

Careful, Hart warned herself. Careful. "It's not my business to approve or disapprove," Hart told her, trying to keep any trace of emotion out of her voice. "You're a BioStrike officer — I don't know how you're supposed to enforce the Edicts. And California is your state. Things are, well, different in Arizona."

"Quite right," Valentin said.

Hart relaxed a little.

"California is at war, Hart," Valentin told her. "In fact, all of America is. But our enemy is not only the Red Death."

"I don't understand," Hart said, playing the part of the pupil.

"I didn't think you would," Valentin told her. "You don't have enough of the facts to understand. Not yet." She smiled. "Would you like me to tell you some?"

Hart guessed that this was the place where she was supposed to nod and look eager. It didn't require too much effort to feign interest — after all, Valentin might inadvertently tell her something she needed to know. She sat on the floor beside Valentin.

"I thought you'd be interested," Valentin said, ruffling her hair. "All right, my young friend, I'll give you a history lesson. But first, tell me what you know about BioStrike."

"Not much. In December of 2003, something — a biological weapon — was released into the air over America's west coast. Then people started to die. The weapon contained the RD virus — the Red Death."

"Basically correct, but very sketchy. Do we know who released the biological weapon?"

Hart shook her head. "I don't think so. The two theories I hear most often in Tucson are that either the Soviet Union or the Alliance of Islamic States did it."

Valentin nodded. "Either would make a good villain. Unfortunately, neither was responsible."

Hart sat up straight. "Who was, then?"

Valentin smiled again. "You were."

"I was?" Hart blinked furiously, trying to understand.

"I mean you, plural. You Americans."

"Us . . . you mean we did it to ourselves?" Hart whispered.

"Yes."

"How? Why?" Another question occurred to Hart

179

and before she could censor it, she blurted it out.
"And what do you mean, 'you'? Aren't you one of us?
Aren't you an American?"

"Do I sound like one?" Valentin said.

"Well," Hart admitted, thinking of the language
in which Valentin had cursed earlier. "Not really.
What are you then?"

"Let's just say I'm a representative of a friendly
power. Which power really doesn't matter, now does
it? What does matter is that my government has
joined with yours to bring America out of this new
dark age. To restore it to its former greatness."

"But we don't have a government," Hart said.
"We're just a bunch of regional power centers. In
Tucson, we couldn't even make contact with
California for three years."

"That's why we're — I'm — here," Valentin said.
"The BioStrike Force represents the true power in
California. It's an unwritten rule of foreign affairs
that one always seeks to deal with strength."

Hart was trying hard to absorb all this. "Tell me
how we brought BioStrike on ourselves."

Valentin frowned. "That's in the past, Hart.
Ancient history. Are you sure you want to know?"

"I'm sure."

"All right. My government knew you were at
work on a powerful biological weapon. We'd known it
for years." The lines deepened around her mouth.
"And — so I was told — in self-defense, we stole the
formula for the vaccine. We weren't about to be
caught napping if you decided to launch your
biological weapon over our cities. We had to protect
ourselves, after all." She paused. "Your weapon
simply got away from its developers."

"How?" Hart asked. "I've read newspaper accounts and seen videotapes of that time. There was no mention of anything like that. And besides, if your theory is true," she said, realizing something, "then people in power — our government — must have had a vaccine ready. They wouldn't have wanted to accidentally be infected."

"Perceptive, aren't you?" Valentin congratulated Hart. "Yes, of course they *planned* to have the vaccine ready. To have released the virus otherwise would have meant certain death. But — according to the theory — the virus *was* released prematurely. There was an accident — sabotage possibly — and the whole thing blew sky high."

"I don't believe that," Hart said. "It doesn't fit with the facts."

"Facts can be invented, can't they? Grow up." She looked down at Hart. "What does it matter?"

"It matters to me," Hart said heatedly. Valentin's logic infuriated her. "And I think it would matter to others. If it were the truth."

"Anyone who could confirm the theory is long dead, Hart. It's up to people like you — young people — to pick up the pieces. To go on." She placed a hand on Hart's shoulder. "This was once a great country. With our help, you can be great again."

"But the Red Death — what can you do about that?"

"I told you — my government has had a vaccine for years. Once the details of exactly how we are going to render assistance, and how you plan to express your gratitude, have been worked out, why, we'd be more than happy to immunize the RD negatives of America."

181

Something occurred to Hart, and she decided to take advantage of Valentin's expansive mood. "It wasn't the BioStrike Forces who wanted Dr. Ashe, was it? It was you. Your government. But you don't need her — you said yourself that you have a vaccine of your own. So why did you kidnap her? And why did you want her vaccine?"

Valentin smiled secretively. "We have a use for her, never fear."

Hart swallowed. A use? She wondered. And what did Valentin's government really want in return for the help they were going to give? Hart recalled what had happened when California closed its borders. Arizona, cut off from its principal supplier, began to starve. Immediately following BioStrike, more deaths had occurred in Phoenix and Tucson from the sudden shortage of foodstuffs than from the Red Death. Hart frowned. And with the U.S. quarantined, how many nations had suffered the same fate as Arizona? How much good will could the world have toward America?

Valentin looked past Hart, out the window. "This storm shows no signs of letting up," she said. "It's black as night out there. Why don't we try to get some rest? We can eat after we wake up."

"But aren't you worried that some of . . ." she stammered nervously, not knowing what to call the dead man, "his friends might come around? And what about the children he was talking about? The ones who turned him in?"

"It's pouring rain, Hart," Valentin chided. "No one's going to come around here for hours. And believe me, there are no children. The man was clearly unbalanced. I'll set an alarm on my watch so we won't oversleep if it will make you feel better."

"All right," Hart said, wanting only to get away from Valentin. She needed desperately to think.

"Take one of the bedrooms at the back of the house," Valentin said. "I'll take the one here at the front. And I'll sleep with one eye open for callers, don't worry. Although I hardly think there'll be any."

"Fine," Hart said. "And then what?" She had to ask the question, just to hear Valentin's easy lie.

"Then we proceed to BioStrike Central," Valentin told her. "I'll make my report, and your new life will begin. A great day, young Hart. Don't you agree?"

It took all Hart's will power to answer Valentin civilly. "Oh, yes," she said, "I agree."

* * * * *

Hart raised the window as quietly as she could. The drop to the ground was short, but she landed off-balance on the wet grass, slipped, and fell to the ground. Suppressing a curse, she got to her feet and, with one eye on Valentin's bedroom window, sprinted through the rain to the next cabin, squeezing into a narrow space between the woodpile and the house. She leaned, panting, against the rough-cut logs, turning up the neck of her coveralls. The rain was a steady curtain now, and she shivered, unwilling to get drenched. Oh, go on, she told herself. You won't get back to the train this way.

"Going somewhere?" a voice asked from behind a shuttered window.

Hart almost jumped out of her boots. Frantic, she sought the shortest route from the woodpile to the road, and prepared to run.

The barrel of a handgun appeared in the window.

Hart heard the hammer being cocked. "Don't plan on doing any running," the voice said. "You won't get five yards."

Hart looked longingly at the road and woods beyond. "What do you want?" she asked gruffly.

The voice laughed. "Why, you, dearie. That's what we want. You."

A door opened in the cabin and a teenaged boy of about fifteen came out, gun in hand. Hart was appalled at how filthy he was — greasy pants, a shirt that once might have been blue, and long, matted brown hair. Worse than that, though, were the blotchy red patches on his face and neck. Hart swallowed. This boy had the Red Death.

"Get out here, Spider," he called to someone in the cabin behind him.

A skinny dark-haired boy of about twelve came out onto the porch, followed by two other smaller boys and two girls — all thin and dirty, clad in an ill-fitting assortment of clothing.

"Give me your hands," Spider said to Hart, glowering. From a voluminous pocket of his pants, he produced a pair of handcuffs and a chain.

Hart's skin crawled. "No," she told him.

He shook the chain at her. "Give me your hands, bitch, or you'll be sorry. Wolf will do more than suck your blood when we get you tied down." He giggled a little, plainly enjoying this.

She began to edge to her right, trying to put Spider between her and Wolf. "Sucking my blood won't cure Wolf of the Red Death," Hart told Spider. "That's a fairy tale."

Spider looked uncertainly over his shoulder at Wolf.

"Take her," Wolf said impatiently to Spider. "For God's sake, she's just a girl. Or do you want me to show you how to do this, too?"

Spider took one step toward her.

"Has Wolf given you the Red Death yet, Spider?" Hart taunted. "And what about him? I can tell you how long he has to live. Days, Spider. Only days. Who's going to take care of you then?" Bull's eye, she thought, as Spider's hands fell to his sides and his brave advance faltered. She edged a little more to her right. There! At last she had Spider between her and Wolf. In two bounds, she was around the side of the porch. Three more took her behind the cabin. She heard Wolf's enraged shouts, but they only drove her to greater efforts. With a lung-bursting spurt of speed, she rounded the corner of another cabin, the last one between her and the woods, and sprinted for the trees.

The shots came as she ducked behind the massive trunk of a pine, and she crouched, panting, peering back through the undergrowth. Wolf and his ragged little band stood huddled in the rain, looking forlorn in their oversized clothes. Hart saw Wolf kick Spider, then grab one of the children, shaking her by the arm. The new donor, Hart guessed. The child screamed and struggled, but was no match for the bigger boy, and soon she walked along docilely at Wolf's side. One by one the children turned from their contemplation of the forest and trailed along after Wolf, Spider bringing up the rear.

Hart shook her head. She wasn't wasting a moment of sympathy on any of them. They were a pitiful lot, but what could she do?

Collar up, head down against the rain, she came

185

to the road in half an hour of walking. I'll freeze if I don't soon get out of this, she realized, thinking of Valentin snug and warm in the dead man's cabin. Valentin. Just thinking of the other woman made Hart's fists clench. Were all the new BioStrike troopers like her? Valentin could criticize Sandoval and her troopers all she wanted, but they seemed a whole lot more human than Valentin. Hart might never agree with Sandoval's motives, but at least they were understandable.

Sandoval. With grudging acceptance, she had to admit that she no longer hated and feared the remote, intimidating BioStrike Captain. She thought about what Lujan had told her — of how Sandoval had rescued Wilkins, how she had gotten the Sixth out of impossible situations, how her troopers idolized her. She thought about the fact that she too had risked her life to pull Sandoval up the hill. She shook her head. She had known how dangerous the job would be, and had agreed to help Lujan. Saving Sandoval seemed the right thing to do. But on what had she based her decision — her emotions? She would never have risked her life for Valentin. Yet they served the same BioStrike masters, and had the same plans for Ashe and the Gaians.

The rain had stopped. With a start, she looked up through the trees. Blue sky. Valentin would probably be awake — she felt certain the woman was capable of anything. And, finding Hart gone, she would probably have left immediately. She might be only minutes behind. Hart began to run, cutting through the trees to reach the road.

In a moment she reached the clearing where the

SunRaycer was parked. Valentin was not there. Not yet, she told herself, looking nervously inside the plexiglass bubble roof. She eased herself into the driver's seat. Flipping the ignition switch to the ON position, she was gratified to see the instrument panel light up. Now, she thought, her palms sweating, if I can only do this. Easing the gearshift into NEUTRAL, she bit her lip and shoved it into DRIVE. Immediately, a raucous beeping issued from the onboard computer. REQUEST MANUAL OVERRIDE SEQUENCE it informed her in flashing green letters.

"Shit!" she shouted, pounding her fist on the steering wheel in frustration. "I don't have time for this!" Forcing herself to be calm, she entered the computer's PROGRAM mode, and typed in the words MANUAL OVERRIDE. The beeping stopped, and the words SETTING MANUAL OVERRIDE now appeared on the screen. Limp with relief, she got ready, hands on the wheel, foot poised above the accelerator pedal. "Come on, come on," she urged. An interminable ten seconds later, the SunRaycer, too, was ready. MANUAL OVERRIDE COMPLETE, the screen told her. A small green light on the handle of the gear shift lit up, and Hart shifted into DRIVE, frantic to be away. She raised her head to check the road ahead for obstacles . . . and froze in disbelieving terror. There, in the middle of the road, not ten feet from the SunRaycer, stood Valentin, gun drawn, muzzle pointing directly at Hart's head. For one instant, Hart was tempted to floor the accelerator and drive the SunRaycer into and over Valentin. Instead, she shifted back to NEUTRAL, typed JUMP into the computer, and gritted her teeth. Nothing happened.

187

LOW POWER the computer told her. JUMP INADVISABLE. "No!" she shouted. Desperately, she shifted back into DRIVE.

Suddenly the bubble roof was wrenched open and Valentin seized a handful of Hart's hair, holding the pistol to her temple. "You should have killed me when you had the chance," Valentin told her. "Shift back to neutral."

Defeated, Hart obeyed.

Valentin slid the visor of her helmet up and regarded Hart with wintry blue eyes. "A commendable effort," she observed. "But all for nothing."

Hart made no reply. What could she possibly have said? She moved her head a little, wanting to see where the pistol was, thinking she might throw herself at Valentin, but the other woman rapped her painfully on the cheekbone with the gun barrel.

"Don't try anything," Valentin warned. "Just slide over into the passenger seat."

Hart climbed over the gearshift and slumped in the other seat. Valentin took the driver's seat and favored Hart with one meaningful look. Hart closed her eyes, feeling a bleak, hopeless despair. Even inquiring about her fate seemed too onerous a task. Maybe this is all for the best, she told herself. Valentin will take me into the woods and shoot me. At least I won't have to struggle any more. Or worry about the future. Or what I ought to have done and ought not to have done. She looked over at Valentin. The prospect of a bullet through the head seemed somehow appealing.

Valentin put the SunRaycer into DRIVE and began to negotiate the log-choked road, driving now and then into the ditch to avoid the more impossible spots. "Damn," she said. "I'm afraid we'll have to walk to our destination after all. But relax while you can, young Hart," Valentin told her in a voice full of cheerful menace. "You'll soon wish you had succeeded in your escape, or perished in the attempt."

"What do you mean?" Hart asked.

Valentin laughed, a low breathless sound that raised the hair on the back of Hart's neck.

"What I mean, you ineffectual *girl*, is that you are about to buy me safe conduct through the pass. I learned from, ah, judicious questioning of those creatures back at Oak Creek that the pass is held by a force of blood collectors — a grown-up version of those silly children."

Hart's scalp prickled. "What are you going to do?" she asked in horror.

"Why I'm going to sell you to them, of course," Valentin told Hart gleefully. "Do you have any idea what you're worth on the black market — a nice healthy RD negative specimen like you?"

Sickened, Hart shook her head.

Valentin laughed. "No, I'm sure you don't. Well, you're worth a safe conduct — that's for sure. And that's all I really care about. If I have to, I'll throw in the vaccine and the radio as well, but I don't think I'll have to." She glanced at Hart. "You'll bring a good price all on your own."

Tears sprang to Hart's eyes. Despair and self-pity overwhelmed her. Was this why she had been spared three years ago? To die in a blood collectors' camp?

Valentin patted Hart's knee in a parody of concern. "Tut, tut," she said reprovingly. "No sniveling, now. I want you to look your best. After all, if the blood collectors don't want you for your blood, they might want you for something else." She chuckled. "After all — you've been vaccinated. You can't get the Red Death. That opens up all kinds of possibilities, now doesn't it?"

Hart turned her face away and, looking out the window, wished she were dead.

CHAPTER 10

Come not between the Dragon and its wrath.
William Shakespeare, *Othello*

Sandoval put her hand on the hood of the SunRaycer. The engine was still warm. Valentin had evidently tried to hide the vehicle, but it was an amateur effort. Oh, it was concealed well enough from anyone who wasn't looking for it, but Lujan's sharp eyes had spotted it at once. Sandoval lifted the plexiglass bubble and looked inside. There in the cargo hatch was a box. Reaching for it, she hefted it, hardly daring to hope. It was heavy. And the tape around the box's opening hadn't been broken. Beside it, in a waterproof canvas case, lay the radio. Valentin must have been convinced either that no one would follow or that the pursuer would never locate the SunRaycer. Sandoval snorted. "Such arrogance," she muttered under her breath. "We're in luck," she told Lujan, who had appeared at her elbow. "Two out of three."

"But no Hart," Lujan commented quietly. She looked around at the tangle of logs. "They couldn't take the SunRaycer through this, so they walked. But where to? The pass is just beyond those trees. Surely they're not going to walk to Central?"

Sandoval frowned. Valentin would never walk to Central. Therefore, she planned to come back for the SunRaycer — presumably to re-charge it — or planned to acquire other means of transportation. "Let me see the map," she said to Lujan.

"Captain," Lujan said tentatively, "I was just thinking . . ."

"Thinking about what?" she asked, peering at the map. "Tell me. Please. I haven't had any bright ideas of my own."

"Well, wouldn't the pass be a good strategic location for a bandit camp?" Lujan asked. "A small force could control it, and as it's the only way through these mountains, they could demand —"

"Jesus!" Sandoval exclaimed. "Of course. You're a genius, Lujan."

Lujan blushed, and Sandoval turned away quickly so the young woman wouldn't see the smile on her face. She reached into the SunRaycer and handed Lujan the radio. "Hide this in the rocks over there," she told Lujan. "I'll take this box and put it on the other side of the road, in those bushes."

"Is that the vaccine?" Lujan asked, pointing at the container.

Sandoval lifted the box in her arms and held it against her chest. "Yes. A magic bullet," Sandoval observed wryly. "Ashe's Red Death vaccine. Hope, Lujan."

Lujan stood, radio in hand, looking hungrily at the container. An expression of pain crossed Lujan's face, gone in an instant, replaced by an ineffable sadness. Too late, Sandoval realized the mistake she had made. There could be no hope for Lujan. The vaccine was useless to her. For Lujan already had the Red Death. Stupid, Sandoval berated herself. A stupid, thoughtless remark.

But Lujan looked up at Sandoval and smiled bravely. "Good," she said, and turned away.

Sandoval carried the vaccine nearly two hundred meters into the scrubby underbrush. Putting it down carefully behind some thorn bushes, she stood, fists clenched, eyes closed, unwilling to go out and face Lujan. With mortified astonishment, she felt the unfamiliar sting of tears behind her eyes. Fool! she raged. What would your troopers say if they could see you now? The fearsome BioStrike Captain, weeping in the bushes. And for what? One woman's life? Where's your sense of perspective, Sandoval — what can one life mean, anyhow? You've been responsible for the murder of hundreds of people. Perhaps thousands. Most of them were innocent of any crime or wrongdoing. You knew that. Worse, you've committed murder without turning a hair. And lest you totally lose your sense of balance, think of the bigger picture. The Red Death has claimed hundreds of thousands. Life as a singular noun no longer has any meaning.

"No," she said aloud, suddenly, decisively. "It does. It does because it must." And suddenly, things clicked into focus. Ashe, Onava, Irena, her remaining troopers, Lujan, Hart — they had been placed in her care. This knowledge pierced her, and because she knew it was true, she trembled. She, who deserved nothing, had been given a precious gift, and the generosity of fate humbled her. She did not doubt for one instant that she possessed the power to preserve life — after all, she had possessed the power to take it away. What she had needed, had always needed, was for the life she had held so cheaply to become suddenly dear. She had needed life to reach out and take her by the throat, to proclaim its worth. "I won't fail," she whispered, for Ashe, who had asked her to bring Hart back safely, for Lujan who depended on her. And most of all, for herself. "I won't fail."

* * * * *

"What is it?" Lujan asked as they peered out from behind a clump of pines at the edge of the camp. Several large tents had been erected in the center of a clearing, and around them were smaller shelters — tents, lean-tos, even a few battered and rusted automobiles.

"A blood collection camp," Sandoval told Lujan. She swept the camp with her binoculars, but saw no one. Strange. Even the communal cooking fires were unattended. "The renegades who run the camp

194

kidnap people — mostly women and children, although they have been known to raid convents and abbeys. They do their testing in the field, so they only bring RD negatives back here. Then, depending on market conditions, they sell either the entire person or several units of her blood to the nearest BioStrike A & T facility."

"Yeah, I remember hearing about them now," Lujan said.

Sandoval laughed bitterly. "See, Lujan? There are worse jobs than being a corporal in the Sixth."

"Do you think Valentin and Hart are here?"

"Yes, I do," Sandoval said. "What I can't imagine is why."

"Maybe Valentin wants to buy some blood to take to the A & T facility with her," Lujan suggested.

"Unlikely," Sandoval said. "Knowing Valentin, she's probably selling some of hers." A hideous thought occurred to her and she lowered her binoculars, squeezing her eyes closed. "Oh, Jesus. No."

Lujan turned her worried brown eyes on Sandoval. "Hart?"

Sandoval nodded.

Lujan studied the camp through her own binoculars. "That big tent on the right," she said. "There's smoke coming out the top. Probably from a cookstove. I'll bet everyone's in there."

Sandoval looked for herself. "You could well be right," she said. She put the binoculars away, and unholstered her gun. Briefly, she regretted the pistol she had given Ashe. But this was Rincon's pistol — it would work just as well. Still, she couldn't help a twinge of superstitious anxiety as she checked the load. She looked at Lujan, and forced a smile. Once more, she told herself. Just this once more. "Ready, Corporal?"

"Yes, Captain," Lujan said, giving her a sad, trusting smile.

"Listen," she told Lujan fiercely. "We're both coming out of that tent. With Hart. You're damned well not dying here. From a bullet or from the Red Death. Do you believe me?"

Lujan looked into Sandoval's eyes for a long moment. "I'd like to," she whispered huskily.

Sandoval gripped her shoulder. "Then do it. You won't die here because I won't let you. I've lost too many of you, let too many of you down. All right?"

Lujan swallowed, then nodded.

"Come on, then," Sandoval said roughly. "Let's get this over with."

* * * * *

Lujan beside her, Sandoval simply walked through the open door and into the tent. About twenty men sat or lounged in a rough semicircle on a dirt floor, around a raised platform at one end of the tent. In the middle of the semicircle was an iron stove, a pile of wood beside it. On the platform were two middle-aged men, Hart, and Valentin. Valentin and the two men sat on wooden chairs on three sides of a rough table. Hart sat on a stool just to one side of the table. Her hands were tied behind her, Sandoval noted, and there was blood on her chin. Her upper lip was cut and swollen. Sandoval remembered Hart's brashness and guessed that someone had taken offense at one of her remarks and had struck her.

As she and Lujan moved through the small crowd of men, she was gratified to note that a murmuring began, and that legs were drawn aside to let her pass. The mystique of the BioStrike Forces was evidently still alive. However, she would have to be vigilant. Getting in was one thing; getting out, another.

Stopping at the edge of the platform, she tipped up her visor. Lujan fell into place behind her and without looking, she knew that Lujan was covering her back. They had done this sort of thing a dozen times before.

"You have something that belongs to me," she said, addressing the two men on the platform. "I want it back."

"Do you now?" one of the men said. He was dressed in frontier garb, Sandoval noted with amusement. A sort of costume, made from animal skins. Perhaps he thought this made him more frightening. His head was shaved, and around his neck he wore a necklace of small bones, tipped with claws. From his ears hung earrings — twists of wire from which hung tufts of what seemed to be human hair. If the situation hadn't been so perilous, she might have laughed aloud. This man was grotesque.

"Captain Sandoval," Hart said in disbelief. "You're not dead."

"As you see," she told Hart. So that was the ruse Valentin had used to persuade Hart.

"You're too late," the shaven-headed man informed her. "Your junior officer here has just made us a deal for this, ah, commodity." He indicated Hart with a wave of his hand.

"Oh?" Sandoval said. "She had no such authority to do so. That *commodity* is BioStrike property. My

197

orders are to bring her to Los Angeles, to BioStrike Central. Are you telling me that you knowingly intend to prevent me from doing my duty?" She crossed her arms over her chest, making certain her gun hand was on top. The effect was not lost on the frontiersman, whose eyes strayed nervously to her pistol. Sensing an advantage, Sandoval pressed on. "The BioStrike Forces and the collectors have had good relations over the years. I trust you'll do nothing to imperil them."

The frontiersman licked his lips nervously, and looked sidelong at the other man, a quiet, dark-haired man dressed in a heavy green shirt and brown pants. He looked vaguely familiar, but when Sandoval's memory did not produce his name, she gave up. She understood the situation, though. The green-shirted man was the leader, the frontiersman his lieutenant. Presumably Greenshirt was allowing Frontiersman to handle this episode alone as a form of leadership training. Or a test. Battlefield experience, so to speak. She smiled to herself. There was no way Frontiersman could win an exchange with her. Better men — and women too — had tried and failed.

"I, that is, we do want to maintain good relations with the BioStrike Forces," Frontiersman agreed, "but we've made a deal, you see. A bargain. We've given our word. And this officer has given hers." He paused for dramatic effect. "Now you wouldn't want the BioStrike Forces to get the reputation for being unfair or unreliable. Would you?" He grinned, showing dirty, tobacco-stained teeth.

Sandoval decided to ignore this line of debate. She glowered at the man, choosing to reiterate her position a little more forcefully. "You are in illegal

possession of something that is the property of
BioStrike Central," she said, injecting a note of
annoyance into her voice. "Whatever you have given
Lieutenant Valentin for that young woman will be
returned to you. This *commodity* is non-negotiable
property."

The frontiersman smiled and spread his hands.
"Fine," he said. "We'll be happy to take it back."

Some of the men behind Sandoval chuckled, and
she felt the hair on the back of her neck prickle.
Why had he capitulated so easily?

"You ass!" Valentin said, acknowledging
Sandoval's presence for the first time. "You don't
know what you're doing. Let me handle this."

"It's done," Sandoval told Valentin. "Whatever
bargain you've made, you'll have to unmake. And live
with it." Sandoval motioned to Hart with her gun
hand. "Come down here, Hart," she said. Hart sprang
to her feet, jumped from the platform, and hurried to
stand beside Sandoval. "Cut her loose," she told
Lujan.

"Not so fast," the frontiersman said. Lujan
ignored him and cut Hart's bonds.

So, Sandoval said to herself, here comes the
serious resistance.

"Your officer tells us that this girl has been
vaccinated against the Red Death," the frontiersman
said conversationally.

"That's true," Sandoval told him. She saw no
point in denying it.

"Who has the vaccine?" he asked, putty-colored
eyes greedy.

One by one, voices began behind Sandoval.
Desperate voices.

Sandoval smiled, seeing a chance to turn this situation to her advantage. "You'd be better off asking Lieutenant Valentin," she called over her shoulder to the muttering men. "She had the foresight to bring it with her."

Plainly surprised, the frontiersman turned to Valentin. "You didn't tell us you had the vaccine."

"I don't," Valentin said.

"Lieutenant Valentin!" Sandoval exclaimed in feigned astonishment. "What was in that box I found in the SunRaycer, if not vaccine?"

"You *are* a fool," Valentin said menacingly, rising to her feet. "Why couldn't you keep your mouth shut? Now none of us will get out of here!"

"Where's the vaccine?" a man called from the crowd. "Make her give it to us!"

A chorus of voices agreed with him.

Good, Sandoval thought gleefully. Confusion always helps. She reached into the left-hand chest pocket of her coveralls and held up a stoppered vial, securely wrapped in plastic. "Here's a sample," she said to the frontiersman. "For the rest, you'll have to speak to the Lieutenant there." She tossed the vial in a high arc, and he caught it neatly.

The green-shirted man held out a hand, and the frontiersman handed him the vial. "Thank you," Greenshirt said. "Captain Sandoval, isn't it?"

She nodded, memory suddenly supplying a name. "Burke," she said. "Damian Burke."

His eyebrows lifted in surprise. "I thought you'd have been dead long ago."

She smiled. "I'm hard to kill."

He nodded. "Give my respects to Central." He examined the vial briefly. "How do we administer this?"

Sandoval shrugged. "I don't know. Valentin might. Or some of your medical personnel."

Burke nodded again. "You may go," he told her. "We'll just detain Lieutenant Valentin a little longer. There are some questions I'd like to ask her. It appears she wasn't dealing in good faith."

But Valentin was determined to go down fighting, Sandoval saw.

"Idiot!" Valentin screamed at him. "She's playing with you. Kill them. You can have the vaccine and the girl, too. No one will report you."

Burke shook his head. "Tales have a way of traveling," he said. "It makes poor economic sense to risk antagonizing the only buyers of the goods and services one produces. Surely you see that?"

Sandoval decided to act while the spotlight had shifted to Valentin. With any luck, by the time Burke and Valentin had settled their differences, the three of them would be well away from here.

"Fall back, Lujan," Sandoval said, and they began to retreat toward the tent's opening. "Hart, don't leave my side."

"No," Valentin said, moving away from the table. In an instant, she had drawn her pistol and pointed it at Sandoval's chest. "If I do nothing else, I'm going to be rid of you."

Sandoval debated the odds. Could she bring her gun up, cock the trigger, aim, and fire before Valentin squeezed the trigger? She decided she couldn't. So, here it was, she told herself. All these years of hard-fought survival, only to meet death at the hands of another BioStrike officer. A final irony.

"Lujan, get Hart out of here," she said quietly. She didn't wait to see what happened. Taking a deep breath, she began to walk back to the platform.

CHAPTER 11

*They who have courage and faith will never
perish in misery.*

Anne Frank

Time seemed to stop for Hart. She was beyond
shock, beyond drama, beyond climax and anticlimax.
Her system had had one too many blows and buffets.
She was past the ability to think. And that was what
made everything so clear. She still wasn't certain
whether this was a dream, but suddenly it didn't
matter. If it was, she'd wake up and get on with her

life. If it wasn't, she'd regret this for the rest of her life. She sensed Lujan behind her, and it was as if their minds were linked. She seemed to know Lujan's intentions. And so it was necessary that she do her part, too. It was all very simple. Taking two running steps, she wrapped her arms around Sandoval and dragged her to the floor. Lujan's gun went off as she and Sandoval were falling to the ground, and she buried her face in Sandoval's shoulder, deafened, stunned.

Please, she prayed, let this be enough.

"Very pretty," she heard a voice say.

She looked up at Lujan, but the young trooper was silent, gun still extended in front of her, eyes fixed on the platform. It must have been Burke who had spoken, Hart decided.

Sandoval stirred beneath her, and Hart raised her head to look. What had happened to Valentin? There was no longer an angel of death poised on the platform. Instead, she lay on her back, broken, silent, a splash of bright blood staining the left breast of her black uniform. Her pistol lay beside her. Hart rose unsteadily to her feet. "Sorry," she said to Sandoval, offering her a hand.

Rising to her knees, Sandoval seemed to take in everything at a glance — Lujan, Burke, Valentin. Then she rose gracefully to her feet, not needing Hart's hand, but pressing it once, quickly, nonetheless.

"Pretty?" Sandoval asked. She looked at Valentin's body for a long moment, then quickly from Hart to Lujan. "No," she said decisively. She turned her back on Burke, then, putting her arms around

Hart's and Lujan's shoulders, she walked with them out of the tent.

* * * * *

Hart slumped down on the ground beside the SunRaycer, too drained to move. Sandoval said something quietly to Lujan, and the trooper walked off into the bushes. After a moment, Sandoval came to sit beside Hart.

"That was a brave thing you did," she said. "Thank you. Again."

Hart answered mechanically. "You're welcome." Then after a moment's thought, she added, "But it wasn't brave."

"Of course it was," Sandoval told her. "You might have been killed."

Hart was so tired she could hardly speak. But she wanted Sandoval to know the truth. It suddenly seemed important. "I did it because I had to," she said. "Not because I'm brave. Or because I wanted to do it."

"Don't denigrate your actions," Sandoval told her. "That's what courage is all about — the moment when you have nothing else to offer but your life." She looked at Hart earnestly. "Each of us has only one life, Hart. So when the moment comes, you have to be ruthless. If I'm to die, I want to be very sure that what I'm dying for is worth the sacrifice."

Hart closed her eyes. Hadn't she herself said something like this to Medina? How long ago it seemed. "How can you know what's worth dying for?" she asked.

"You know," Sandoval said. "You always know."

Hart considered this, and remembered what Lujan had told her the night they had rescued Sandoval. "I sometimes think there's only one thing worth stirring an inch for," Lujan had said. "And that's love."

She looked at Sandoval. "I'm confused," she said. "I hate what the BioStrike Forces are doing. I hate it that you kidnapped Ashe and me. I hate it that you were responsible for Medina's death. I hate it that you've taken my life at MedCenter away from me." She took a deep breath. "So dammit, why don't I hate you? Why didn't I refuse to help Lujan? Why didn't I let Valentin shoot you?"

Sandoval looked away. "I don't know, Hart," she said. "You'll have to answer those questions for yourself." After a moment's silence, she turned to Hart again. "I just want you to know that when we get back to the others, I'll find a way to take Ashe someplace safe and you back to Tucson."

Hart hadn't intended to laugh, but a bitter, choked sound escaped her. "That's like what Valentin told me at first," she said to Sandoval. "That she'd take me to BioStrike Central. That they would listen, and would send me home. I even believed her for awhile."

"BioStrike Central would never have sent you home," Sandoval told her. "They'd have put you in a donor camp. No, Hart, I said *I* would get you back to Tucson. And I will."

Hart rested her head against the side of the SunRaycer. "But don't you see?"

"See what?"

"I can't go home," Hart told her in a voice that sounded thin even to her. As soon as the words were

206

out of her mouth a vast desolation came over her, a terrible sense of abandonment. She closed her eyes, fighting back tears.

"Why on earth can't you go home?" Sandoval demanded.

Hart wiped her sleeve over her eyes. "Tucson administrators knew all about Ashe's kidnapping," Hart said. "I overheard them talking about it. For all I know, they *planned* it! They certainly cooperated in its execution. So they won't exactly be glad to see me back, knowing what I know."

"Dammit," Sandoval said, half to herself. "I realized Ashe wouldn't be welcome back in Tucson. I forgot about you."

"I'll have to take care of myself, I guess," Hart said. Suddenly, something that Valentin had told her tugged at her mind. She looked at Sandoval. "I thought I knew the truth about BioStrike. But Lieutenant Valentin —"

"Valentin!" Sandoval snorted. "Valentin had her own agenda. I'm sure she wouldn't have hesitated to tell you anything."

Hart nodded. "She implied that, well, that America brought BioStrike on itself. That the west coast explosion which started the Red Death was really the explosion of some biological warfare facility."

Sandoval laughed softly. "So that's the official propaganda statement, is it?"

"What do you mean?" Hart asked. "And by the way, where *was* she from anyhow?"

Sandoval snorted again. "We have a lot of enemies. Who can be sure? South America? The Islamic States? Or one of the Communist nations —

Cuba, Nicaragua, East Germany? I'm tempted to think that she took her orders from Moscow, but that's just my opinion. In any event, she told you what her masters have decided we will believe." She paused, thoughtful. "You know, I've been doing some thinking about our friend Valentin," she added. "I believe I've finally figured out what she was up to."

"Oh?"

"I think she was sent to the Sixth to assassinate Ashe and destroy the vaccine."

Shocked, Hart was unable to speak for a moment. "But . . . why?"

"Simple. Her country has a vaccine. We've known that for a little while. But they can hardly appear to be the Republic of California's saviors if they offer us something we already have. If we're going to give them a toehold in America, they'll have to give us something we need pretty badly."

Hart was appalled. "But Arizona . . . they *sent* Ashe to the BioStrike Forces. Did they know that California was about to enter into some kind of agreement with a foreign power?"

Sandoval shook her head. "My guess is they didn't. And don't forget — the BioStrike Forces and the Provisionary Government are now no longer working together. I wouldn't be surprised if certain elements in the BioStrike Forces stage a coup and take power. With a little help from their friends, of course."

Hart felt ill. "Well, Valentin did get the vaccine, but she didn't get Dr. Ashe. She didn't even try."

"Oh?" Sandoval asked. "Didn't she? Do you think that tree across the tracks was an accident? I don't."

208

Aghast, Hart looked at Sandoval. "But why cause so many unnecessary deaths?"

Sandoval shrugged. "Why not?"

Hart suddenly remembered Valentin's cold-blooded murder of the man in the cabin at Oak Creek. Yes, Valentin could have engineered the train wreck. Such a person was capable of anything.

"It still doesn't make sense," Hart said faintly, shaking her head.

"It doesn't have to," Sandoval said. "It's politics."

Politics. Hart closed her eyes. "You know, what I'd really like is just to go home. To forget all this. But I can't. I don't have one."

Suddenly Sandoval started to laugh. "Well, Hart, that makes at least three of us."

"What do you mean?"

Sandoval wiped tears from her eyes. "Ashe, you, and me. None of us can go home."

"You? Why can't you go home? Or back to headquarters or wherever you live?"

Sandoval stood up, stretching. "Because I've committed treason. I've disobeyed the BioStrike Edicts." She smiled down at Hart. "And I intend to keep on disobeying them."

Hart stared up at her. For her and Ashe to be refugees was one thing. But Sandoval?

"Then what will you do?" Hart asked.

Sandoval shrugged. "I don't know. I haven't thought that far ahead. I have my promise to fulfill to the Gaians, and to Ashe and you. And I have an obligation to my troopers. Afterwards . . ." She shrugged again.

Suddenly it seemed right to tell Sandoval what was on her mind. "After Valentin killed a man at

Oak Creek, an idea came into my head. A plan. It was all there, all the parts. I hadn't realized how much I wanted to do it until then."

"To do what?"

"You'll laugh, but I don't care who laughs any more. I'm going to find Sanctuary. And I think I know how to do it. I think I know the missing piece of the puzzle."

"You and Lujan," Sandoval said sadly. "You're two of a kind. Romantic dreamers. Captivated by that myth."

"I don't think it's a myth," Hart protested. "I've heard the radio transmissions at night. And Lieutenant Valentin didn't think it was a myth, either. She had me take an aerial up a tree in order to bring in a line-of-sight broadcast. She seemed to accept as fact that somewhere an enclave of women existed who were free of BioStrike control. Of course, she was opposed to the idea. But she was determined to locate them just the same."

Sandoval looked at Hart in surprise. "Was she? Did she think Sanctuary was someplace nearby?"

Hart tried to recall what Valentin had said. "Not very nearby. In the state, anyhow. On the north coast, I think." Hart turned to Sandoval excitedly. "I've thought a little about this, and the signals must be sent by repeaters. If that's true, then there's a whole network of women out there broadcasting, telling other women about Sanctuary."

"Hart," Sandoval said sympathetically, "even if this were true, I can't imagine how we'd find the place."

"I think I can find it," Hart said. "I —"

Lujan stepped out of the bushes, the radio in its

canvas case in one hand, the container of remaining vaccine in the other. "You can?" she asked, her eyes telling Hart how badly she wanted to believe this.

Hart swallowed. "I think so." It was on the tip of her tongue to tell Lujan and Sandoval about the bold plan she had made at Oak Creek, but common sense prevailed. One thing at a time, she reminded herself.

"How?" Lujan asked, loading the radio and vaccine into the SunRaycer.

Hart felt herself blushing. "I . . . well . . . first we need to go back to where you left the others. I have to talk to Irena."

"The crazy woman?" Sandoval asked, amazed.

"Yes."

Sandoval looked at Hart as if she, not Irena, might be the madwoman. "All right," she said. "But before we do, there's something I have to ask you, Hart. A favor."

Hart looked at Sandoval, puzzled. "What?"

"No, Captain," Lujan said admonishingly.

Sandoval frowned at the young corporal. "No interruptions, Corporal Lujan. This is between Hart and me." She turned to Hart. "Lujan needs a transfusion from an O positive donor. She's RD positive, Stage One. The train wreck took care of the blood I harvested a few days ago. Your blood, Hart. I'm sorry to have to ask you, but I have no choice."

The Red Death. After all this, Hart thought. After all we've been through, it comes back to the damned Red Death. Will we never be free of this curse?

With a shake of her head, Lujan turned her back on the two of them. "You had no right to ask that," Lujan said in a tight voice.

"Perhaps not," Sandoval agreed. "But we're not debating philosophy, Lujan. We're talking about your life."

For Hart, there was virtually no decision to be made. They had risked their lives for each other on the hillside. Hart knew she would do so again if necessary. Giving Lujan her blood seemed to formalize the bond between them. "I'll do it, Lujan," she said. "You should know that."

"Hart," Lujan said, turning to face her. "Be sure. You know how you felt about it last time."

"It was taken from me last time. But a lot has happened since then. I don't want you to die, dammit. If my blood will keep you alive, of course you can have it. Besides, don't I owe you that much? You saved my life."

"Thank you," Lujan said formally.

Sandoval cleared her throat. "Come on, you two. We can't stand around here all day. We'll do the transfusion as soon as we get back. But first we have to get both these vehicles back there. And hope we can find where Rincon and Onava hid the entrance to that canyon."

PART THREE
SANCTUARY

CHAPTER 12

What thou lovest well remains — the rest is dross.
What thou lovest well shall not be reft from thee.
What thou lovest well is thy true heritage.
                                        Ezra Pound, "Canto LXXXI"

Sandoval paced up and down outside the
MedCenter van, waiting for Ashe. Finally the doctor
emerged, stripping off her disposable gloves and
dropping them in a trash bin bolted to the side of
the van marked "Infectious Materials — Use Extreme
Caution."

"She'll be all right," Ashe told her. "They're young and healthy. Well, relatively healthy. They'll both be all right."

Sandoval relaxed a little, stopped her pacing, and leaned against a tree in the twilight. "Thank you."

Ashe fiddled with the velcro closure of one pocket. "I did very little. Hart supplied the blood."

She's avoiding looking at me, Sandoval realized. Why? "Doctor," she said quietly. "What's wrong?"

Ashe raised her bright blue eyes to Sandoval's, and to her immense surprise, Sandoval saw tears there. "I want to show you something," Ashe said.

"All right."

"This way," Ashe said, pointing to a little trail that led into the forest. Sandoval fell into step beside her, and they walked along in companionable silence. "This valley is a wonderful spot," Ashe commented as the tall pines closed around them. "Rincon and Estefan couldn't have picked a better place if they'd tried. There's a lake, a waterfall, meadows, a forest. There are fish in the lake and birds and animals in the woods. The whole place is so *alive*," Ashe said. She chuckled a little. "You know, Onava and the Gaians maintain that we were led here. That the earth mother wanted us to find this place."

"Hmmmph," Sandoval said, trying hard to sound skeptical. "Onava will have us all talking to trees if we're not careful."

"Might not be a bad idea," Ashe said. "Watch your footing. It's rocky here. We're coming to the lakeshore — just over that rise."

They topped the rise, and from the rocky hill, Sandoval looked out over the lake. She blinked, and a feeling of déjà vu came over her, a feeling so

216

powerful it made her tremble. "I . . ." she began, but she could only look. From far away, she heard Ashe call her name, but she was powerless to reply. I know this place, she thought.

Across the lake was an alpine meadow. Grasses grew knee-high, reaching from the forest's edge down to the shore. At the intersection of trees and grass, three deer stood motionless, heads raised. A little waterfall at the lake's far end poured over a cliff and emptied into a pool. Two small bats, fluttering like butterflies, dipped down to skim mouthfuls of water from the pool. In the forest behind her a screech owl whistled, a soft, hollow sound, repeated slowly, ending in a tremulous trill.

This is the valley I saw in my dream, she thought. The valley I was *shown*. She blinked, and came back to reality.

"Captain," Ashe said, putting a hand on her arm. "Are you all right?"

Sandoval sighed. "Finally, yes." She turned to look at Ashe. "Would you believe me if I told you that I saw this place in a dream? The night Lujan and Hart hauled me up out of the train wreck?"

Ashe nodded. "I'd believe you."

"I didn't understand then," Sandoval told her. "I knew I was being shown this valley for some purpose, but I couldn't decipher the message. I know now." She took a deep breath. "Perhaps Onava is right. Gaia may well have led us here."

Ashe looked skeptical. "I'd prefer to believe that Captain Sandoval led us here, by whatever roundabout means." She turned to look out over the lake, hands in the pockets of her coveralls. "However we came here, it's the most beautiful place I've seen in years. Your troopers think so too, Captain. Do you know that they took a vote? They want to stay here until the wounded are well."

Sandoval wasn't surprised. "And then?"

Ashe turned to Sandoval and smiled. "Can't you guess? They want to go wherever it is you're going."

"Fools," Sandoval replied, aware that her voice had become husky. "They should go back to Central. They'll be outlaws if they desert."

"They know that," Ashe said quietly. "But they want to stay with you. They love you, Captain."

Sandoval felt small, humble. "They shouldn't," she whispered. "I taught them to murder and kidnap. I've made monsters of them. They've lost their souls because of me. Whatever good I might do the rest of my life can never atone for these last three years."

Ashe stepped in front of Sandoval and scowled at her. "Don't say that," she said fiercely. "Your troopers aren't brutes. There's not a monster among them. What they, and you, did was wrong. But that's over now. My God, Captain — your troopers aren't stupid. They know something worth loving when they see it."

Sandoval looked into Ashe's eyes. "Then they're mistaken, Doctor."

"No," Ashe said. "They aren't." She was so close Sandoval heard her breathing. "Really, Sandoval. You're like a bloody armadillo. Your troopers want to love you. They need to. Let them."

"I can't," she said.

"Of course you can," Ashe told her. "All you have to do is want to."

Sandoval held her breath, quite aware that Ashe was telling her more about her own feelings than

218

about her troopers' affections. I do want to, she said to herself. But I'm afraid of love. It carries too much responsibility with it. "I'll try," she told Ashe. "That's all I can promise to do."

Ashe laughed, a low, melodious sound in the darkness. "Good," she said. "By the way, do you have a first name?"

Now it was Sandoval's turn to laugh. "Of course. It's Zia."

"Zia," Ashe said, trying it out. "I like it. Mine's Jean, by the way."

I know, Sandoval thought, saddened. I read it in my orders. The orders instructing me to kidnap you. "Thank you," she said.

"It's going to be pitch dark here soon," Ashe said. "Let's go back before we fall and break something. I don't need any more patients."

Sandoval suddenly remembered Hart. And the radio. "I'd like you to hear something," she said, hoping Hart wouldn't mind a little company while she listened for the sounds of Sanctuary. "Your young friend Hart has proven to be a most resourceful person. I'm curious to see whether she can surprise us one more time."

CHAPTER 13

Well I'm sending out this signal, hear?
Hope you can pick it up loud and clear.

Joni Mitchell,
"You Turn Me On, I'm a Radio"

"Be careful," Hart called to Lujan. "It's so dark I don't know how you can see what you're doing. Besides, you shouldn't be up there anyhow. You should be resting. Ashe will skin me alive when she finds out I've let you up."

"I'm just finished," Lujan called from the

branches of the pine tree. "It took a few minutes to get the aerial to stay in place." She hung from the lowest branch of the pine, then dropped to the ground. "All done."

Angry with herself for not having stopped Lujan from climbing the tree, Hart stepped toward the trooper.

"You need to take it easy more than I do," Lujan told her. "After all, you're the one who gave blood."

"Will you please be careful?" Hart asked lamely, putting one hand on Lujan's arm.

"All right," Lujan said. "I just didn't want you to think I'm . . . an invalid."

"I don't think that," Hart said, aware of the hard muscles in Lujan's arm. "I don't think that at all."

Lujan looked at Hart for a long moment. "I've been meaning to say something to you. Remember the night we brought Captain Sandoval up the hill, when we were in the van together?"

Hart felt her face burning. "Yes."

"I told you that if I had a last wish, it would be to . . . kiss a woman again. Remember?"

"I remember."

Hart heard her take a deep breath.

"I told you I couldn't do it because I'd kill her, and you said —"

"I said that you wouldn't kill me," Hart interrupted, heart beating faster. "But I wasn't sure you'd heard me."

"I heard you," Lujan said in a whisper. "But what did you —"

Quickly, before she lost her nerve, Hart bent forward and kissed Lujan's lips. "Hold me," she murmured.

Lujan hesitated for only a moment, then put her arms around Hart's waist, drawing her close. As Lujan's arms tightened around her, she sensed the terrible yearning in Lujan. But surely it could be no greater than her own.

"I know I'm not about to die from the Red Death," Hart said shakily. "But every morning since my parents died, I've thought 'This is it. This will be the day that *I* die.' *I'm* scared, Lujan."

"I'm scared too," Lujan said. "I've just never admitted it before."

Hungrily, impatiently, Hart reached up and took Lujan's face in her hands. "I don't care what this means. Does that sound awful? Who knows what might happen to us? Tomorrow a force of BioStrike troopers from Central might find us. Or those blood collectors. Or bandits. All I know is that I want this. I want you. Now. There may not be a tomorrow."

"I want you, too, Hart." Lujan drew a tremulous breath. "You're sure about the vaccine, are you? Absolutely sure?"

Hart drew Lujan's face to hers. "I'm sure," she whispered.

Lujan groaned, then parted Hart's lips with her own, her tongue insistent. Hart felt a shock of pleasure — no one had ever kissed her like that. She felt Lujan's hand on her hips, drawing her closer, and she stepped forward, pressing her body to Lujan's. The whole length of her body where it touched Lujan's seemed on fire, and when Lujan put her hands on Hart's breasts, Hart felt incandescent.

Lujan knelt, pulling Hart down beside her. In the dying firelight, Hart saw Lujan's eyes shining, and suddenly a kaleidoscope of Lujan-images flashed

222

through her mind: Lujan with Sandoval on the station platform; Lujan begging Hart for help with Sandoval the night of the train crash; Lujan's hand grabbing hers when she was about to go over the edge of the ravine with the smashed boxcar; Lujan stepping between Sandoval and Valentin.

"I've never done this," Hart said. "But I'm glad my first time is with you."

Lujan put one hand behind Hart's neck, and Hart closed her eyes, trembling. Lujan's hand found the fastenings on Hart's coveralls and she pulled open two of the snaps. Hart gasped as she felt Lujan's hands, then her lips, on her skin. Lujan tugged open the remaining snaps and Hart drew Lujan's curly head to her breasts.

"I can't . . . do this . . . slow," Lujan gasped, her hands gripping Hart's hips. "Not this time."

Hart said nothing as under Lujan's lips, a slow hot tide built up inside her. At last, she thought. At last. Life won't cheat me of this, too.

Lujan's hands moved inside Hart's coveralls, and Hart felt the other woman's warm palms on the sensitive skin of her stomach and thighs. She felt as though she might faint from desire. She gripped Lujan's hair tightly, hardly able to bear her touch, and as the other woman's hand moved down Hart's stomach, parted her thighs and hesitated at her hot, wet center, Hart shuddered. Moving impatiently, she rose to meet the other woman's hand. Lujan said something inarticulate, touched her with tentative fingers, then thrust into her. Hart cried aloud at this intense pleasure.

Lujan raised her face to Hart's, looking at her for a moment in wonder. Then she kissed Hart, her

223

tongue at first gentle, then insistent as her fingers inside Hart began a measured cadence. Hart put her arms around Lujan and, moaning, opened herself to her. The hot tide she had felt earlier built quickly to a pitched agony of sensation, and Hart simply abandoned herself to it. Blind, deaf, oblivious to anything but the urgency of her desire, she felt herself swept along on a molten wave of sensation unlike any she had ever known. And when the wave suddenly crested, she cried out, feeling an explosion in her blood, seeing fireworks behind her closed eyelids. Thank you, she said silently to Lujan, to life, to destiny, to whomever watched over them. Thank you.

* * * * *

"I'll go round up the others while you get the radio ready," Lujan said, rising to her knees and drawing Hart up beside her. "And we need more wood for the fire. But first, I want to say something." She reached out a hand and caressed Hart's hair.

Hart said nothing, listening.

Lujan traced Hart's lips with her fingers. "We're both frightened. So let's watch out for each other. I'm already your sister, you know. I've got your blood in me." Lujan's dark eyes were enormous, and Hart saw how serious she was. "We're blood sisters. In my old neighborhood, and in prison, too, that was the biggest gift we could give each other. I'd like to give you that, Hart."

Hart swallowed, her throat suddenly dry. "Lujan,

224

I'm not . . . I mean, maybe you should pick someone else."

"I can't," Lujan said matter-of-factly. "Like I said, I've got your blood in me."

"I'm not brave enough, Lujan," Hart whispered. "I'd only let you down."

"I don't think you would," Lujan said. "Not if you knew I'd be right there covering your back." She put her hands on Hart's shoulders. "What do you say?"

Hart shook her head in wonder. "I'd like to say yes. But before I do, you have to know something. I started to tell you and the Captain just before she asked me to give you my blood. Do you remember?"

"I guess not," Lujan said ruefully. "A lot was happening then."

"It's about Sanctuary. I decided that if I can get the women to talk to me, to tell me where they are, well, I want to try and find it. I want to go there, Lujan, and I'll take anyone along who wants to come."

"Hart!" Lujan exclaimed.

"Surprised?" Hart asked. "So am I. I don't think I'd make a good leader. But this is something I've been planning ever since Valentin shot that man at Oak Creek. What you said, about being blood sisters, it makes sense," Hart said. "I'd like to know someone was watching out for me. But I'm going to Sanctuary, Lujan. Is that what you want?"

"It's not as real to me as it is to you," Lujan said. "You've actually heard their radio transmissions. But if it exists, yes, I'd like to go there. And here's something for you to think about. Captain Sandoval

225

has pledged our services to Onava and the Gaians, and to you and Ashe. She's promised to take you wherever you want to go. So if you want to go to Sanctuary, it seems as though you'll have lots of company. Me included." She squeezed Hart's shoulders. "Shall we go as blood sisters?"

"I can't think of anyone I'd rather have watching out for me," Hart said. "Yes. Let's go as blood sisters."

* * * * *

Hart uncoiled the wire, connected the antenna to the shortwave radio, and sat down beside it. What Valentin had said about the radio was certainly true — it was antiquated. But Hart knew they were lucky to have even these old relics. In the first year of the Red Death, vandals, anti-technology advocates, and back-to-the-earth types had systematically smashed most electronic equipment. Only here and there, in overlooked warehouses, a few old radios remained.

Hart looked up to see Lujan toss some logs on the fire. She lowered herself to the ground beside Hart, smiling, the firelight making a copper halo behind her hair. Blood sisters. Hart was surprised at how right it seemed.

"I couldn't find Onava or the Gaians or Rincon or Estefan," Lujan said, ticking the names off on her fingers. "Lau is on guard duty, and the Captain and Dr. Ashe should be here any minute."

"I wonder where Onava and her women are," Hart said. "I wanted them to hear this."

Hearing a noise behind them, Lujan turned, then jumped to her feet. "Captain," she said, sketching a

226

salute. "Dr. Ashe. You're just in time — Hart's about to bring in Sanctuary."

"Do you have enough light?" Sandoval asked, eyeing the fire. "We could get more wood."

"Lujan just put some logs on it. They should catch in a minute," Hart said, trying to sound confident. But her mouth was dry. What if it didn't work? What if she was wrong? What would happen to the rest of her plan, her dream? It all depended on being able to locate Sanctuary. Just calm down, she told herself. She knew the voices were there. First thing to do was to bring them in. She flipped on the power switch, and found the two-meter band. Searching through it once, quickly, she was unable to hear anything. Dismayed, she adjusted her headphones and tried again, more slowly this time.

"I've got it," she told the others. "I know it's them. But what they're saying — it doesn't make any sense." She shrugged. "It seldom does. I was hoping tonight would be different."

"Let us hear it," Sandoval said. "Maybe we can make some sense of it."

"Come closer," she told them. "Their signal is weak. This is the best I can do."

Ashe and Sandoval moved closer until all four of them were huddled around the radio.

"All right," she said. "Listen." She adjusted the signal, then sat back.

A faint voice, sibilant with static, strengthened, then spoke to them. *"O Atthis, how I loved thee in the long ago,"* it said, then faded in a hiss.

"Dammit," Hart cried. "The reception is terrible. It's always like this. But sometimes they even say the word 'Sanctuary,' " she explained. "So I know it's them, even though they seem to be talking nonsense. It must be a code."

"It's no code," Sandoval said. "It's a line of poetry."

"Poetry?" Hart asked.

"A fragment from one of Sappho's poems." Sandoval looked embarrassed. "Sappho was a lesbian poet. She lived about six hundred years before the birth of Christ. I read her poems in college," she explained. "When I was young and impressionable. For some reason they stayed with me."

"Will they answer if, say, we give them another line of poetry?" Ashe suggested.

"Maybe," Hart said excitedly. "Maybe they didn't answer before because I didn't know what to say to them."

"Try it," Lujan suggested, bending forward eagerly.

"But I don't know any of that poetry," Hart said.

Sandoval looked up, firelight making her face all planes and angles. She smiled. "I do," she told Hart. "When you get ready, I'll give you a line."

Hart's hands shook as she made the adjustments. "Another of the problems is that we don't have a call sign," she said. "I always just gave my name, hoping they'd answer. But no one did."

"What's so important about a call sign?" Lujan asked.

"Well, all shortwave operators have call signs," Hart explained. "They're meaningful — they tell other operators which state you're from and so on. I tried making one up, but it didn't work." She looked at the trio of faces. "My theory is that there's a secret network of known call signs, and that these people won't answer any operator who can't come up with the right one."

"Dammit," Lujan said in frustration.

"We'll try the poem first," Sandoval said. "Then worry about the call sign."

"All right," Hart said. "Here goes. We'll send the signal in code first and see what happens. Then we'll switch to voice." She wiped her sweaty palm and began to send in Morse Code. "CQ CQ CQ CQ CQ DE HART HART HART BT VOICE." She turned to the women. "I hailed them five times, the way you're supposed to, identified myself three times, then told them to expect a voice transmission. Captain, just speak into the microphone."

Sandoval shrugged, and bent forward. *"The moon has set, and the Pleiades; it is midnight, and time passes, and I sleep alone."* She looked at Hart. "That's it."

Hart turned back to the set. Putting her finger on the code key, she sent "HART AR K." Then she turned the set to RECEIVE, and waited. For a few frustrating moments, there was nothing. Then, the headset began to beep. "My God," Hart said. "They're answering." She clamped the set on her head and listened. "HART HART HART DE YL RPT QRZ QRZ," the Morse message said.

Lujan crowded close to Hart. "What did they say?"

Hart took the headset off, stunned. "They *answered*," she said in wonder. They said: 'Hart — women calling. Please repeat your message. Who are you?' " She took a deep breath. "Now they want the call sign. Something they can recognize." Her heart began to beat faster; her mouth felt dry.

"But you said you didn't know the call sign," Sandoval said reasonably.

"No," Hart told her, "I said that I didn't know it when I used to try to contact these women from MedCenter."

"Well," Ashe said. "What's different now?"

"What's different?" Hart asked. "Irena. I think Irena knows the call sign. That's why I wanted to talk to her again."

"Irena?" Lujan asked, blinking. "Hart, even if she did, she couldn't tell you."

"I think she already has," Hart said quietly, putting the headset back on. "She told me every time I talked to her. But I didn't listen. After Valentin sold me to Burke, suddenly a lot of things crystallized in my mind. I realized then that I already knew the call sign. I really didn't need to talk to Irena, but I wanted to be sure." She wiped her palm again and began to send. "YL YL YL DE HART TKS QRZ VOICE AR K." She left the headset on, and explained the Morse Code message to the other women. "I called the women, I identified myself, and thanked them for their call. Then I told them I'd identify myself in voice transmission."

"Why?" Ashe asked curiously. "Didn't you say that call signs are meant to be sent in code?"

"Yes," Hart said, "but this is a call sign we want to keep secret. If I blurt it out over the air, and it's right, anyone listening will know."

"How can you keep it secret?" Lujan asked. "Whether you tell them in code or in voice, you still have to tell them."

"Sssh!" Hart said. She put her hands on the headset and listened: "HART DE YL GA VOICE QRZ

230

AR K." She took a deep breath. "They said: 'Hart —
women calling. Go ahead with your voice
identification.' "

"Well," Ashe said. "Go ahead."

"I will," Hart said, "I have to think of just how
to say it, though." She closed her eyes for a moment.
"All right, I'm ready." Picking up the microphone,
she said in as firm a voice as she could, "This is
Hart calling. I repeat, this is Hart calling. Please
acknowledge. Over." She flipped the dial to
RECEIVE, and waited.

"We hear you, Hart," the faint voice said. "Please
continue. Over."

Hart turned the dial to SEND, and continued.
"I'd like to send you my call sign, but I wonder if
you can understand me? Is my message clear? Am I
too hard, or am I too easy? Please acknowledge.
Over." She held her breath.

No one moved. It was as if everyone had stopped
breathing. Hart shivered, waiting. In the meadow
behind her, the crickets sounded impossibly loud. The
wind moaned a little in the trees. Finally, the headset
beeped. Hart closed her eyes, concentrating on the
message, listening. "MI2EZE MI2EZE MI2EZE DE YL
BT RST 599 599 BT QRX 1100 TMW QRZ 88 AR
K."

Hart tore the headset off her ears and threw it
into the air, whooping. "Irena was right! We did it!"

Lujan grabbed her. "Tell us what they said!"

"They said: MI2EZE, this is the women calling.
Your signal is excellent, repeat, excellent. We'll call
you tomorrow at eleven p.m. with our call sign.
Goodbye."

"Jesus!" Ashe said. "Is it possible?"

231

"What's this 'Am I too easy?' stuff," Lujan demanded. "That's what Irena says. What is it?"

"The call sign," Hart told them. "MI2EZE. Irena must have been in a group which had a shortwave radio. A group in contact with other women. Perhaps they were on their way to Sanctuary. Somehow, she remembered their call sign. But in her mind, it became garbled."

"Quite a job of deduction," Sandoval said, chuckling.

"Thank you," Hart replied, feeling pleased and shy at the same time. She shut off the power to the radio, and unhooked it from the OLV's battery. "We need to take all this in out of the weather. It shouldn't get wet."

Suddenly, from the darkness came the sounds of running feet. A voice called, "Captain Sandoval!" and as Hart watched, suddenly frightened, Lau came staggering into the firelight.

CHAPTER 14

We shall not cease from our exploration
And the end of all our exploring
Will be to arrive where we started
And know the place for the first time.
                    T. S. Eliot, "Little Gidding"

As Lau fell into Sandoval's arms, two thoughts went through her head at once: that their safe harbor, their sanctuary, had been discovered; and that the sticky wetness on the back of Lau's shirt was surely blood.

"Hart! Run to the vans and get Montalvo!" Ashe ordered. "Tell her Lau's hurt. And get some more wood on the fire, Lujan."

"Captain," Lau grimaced, as Sandoval lowered her to the ground. "It's just my shoulder. But I need to tell you about the riders I saw."

Sandoval set her lips in a grim line. "Tell me, Lau."

"Just about sundown, I was watching from the cliff when I saw a party of half a dozen or so men on horseback ride up the road. They were headed toward the pass. Just then that crazy woman, Irena, came out of the woods and stood in the middle of the road, laughing."

"Irena? I thought she was with Onava."

Lau grimaced in pain as Ashe peeled her shirt away from her shoulder. "She must have wandered off," Lau said.

"She did," a voice said from behind them.

Sandoval turned to see Onava and Rowan stride into the circle of amber light.

"We saw what you did," Onava told Lau. "It was futile, but thank you."

Sandoval thought she might shout from frustration. Everyone but she seemed to know what had happened. "Continue, Lau," Sandoval said tersely. Out of the corner of her eye she saw Ashe's assistant Montalvo come running. Lujan appeared, too, with an armload of wood.

"Yes, Ma'am," Lau said. "The riders stopped, and one of them dismounted. He grabbed Irena and started shaking her. I had already worked my way down to the road and was behind a bunch of boulders, pretty close to them. The rider couldn't get

234

any sense out of Irena, so he threw her down in the rocks on the other side of the road. The other riders had dismounted and were standing around talking, trying to decide what to do. While they were busy, I crossed the road and circled around behind them. Irena was lying in the ditch, crying, and I whispered to her. She recognized me, and was just about to get up and come to me when one of the riders saw me. I grabbed Irena, but between the men yelling and me telling her to be quiet, she was too frightened to cooperate. I picked her up and ran for it, but someone shot me."

"This is not a bullet wound, young lady," Ashe said.

"No, Ma'am," Lau agreed. "It was made by a hunting arrow. One of the aluminum ones — from a crossbow, I think. It went right through — didn't hit anything solid. I heard it go *ping* on the rocks ahead of me." Sandoval heard Lau take a ragged breath. "It knocked me to my knees, and then another arrow hit me. Or would have hit me if I hadn't had Irena slung over my shoulder. I figure it hit something serious because she gave one shriek and went limp. I fell over and dropped her then." She paused, then continued in a much lower voice. "Most of that blood on my back is Irena's. I tried to pick her up again, but someone made a dive for me and I was busy trying to get free. When I finally kicked him in the face, there were two others right there. I had to run. I'm sorry, but I left Irena there. The men chased me for about a mile, and I deliberately led them away from the valley, down toward the river."

"You saw this?" Sandoval asked Onava.

"It's my fault," Rowan said quickly. "Irena was

with me. We were harvesting greens. One minute she was there and the next minute she wasn't. I looked everywhere in the valley. Then I went to get Onava and we decided to look out on the road. We were on top of the cliff. We saw most of it."

"It's not as bad as I thought, but with our luck you'll probably get tetanus," Ashe said, taking some gauze from Montalvo and examining the exit wound on Lau's shoulder.

Lau stoically endured Ashe's probing, then turned to Sandoval. "Captain, what about Irena? We have to go back and find out, don't we? She might be alive. We can't just leave her there."

Sandoval stood up, feeling fatalistic, powerless. It was all happening again. There was to be no peace after all, it seemed. Ah well, she told herself, it had been a pleasant illusion while it lasted. "Of course we do," she said. "But the 'we' will not include you, Private Lau. If you can stand the Doctor's ministrations, presumably you can walk. Get yourself patched up. Onava and Rowan can show us where to look."

* * * * *

As the sun rose, Sandoval scanned the road with her binoculars. There seemed to be no one in sight. The sand bore the marks of fresh hoof prints, but no riders were in evidence. She listened carefully, but there were no noises on the dawn breeze save for the sounds of awakening birds.

"Are you sure I can't persuade you to stay here?" Sandoval asked Ashe.

"Certainly not," Ashe said. "If that woman needs

236

medical attention, the sooner she receives it, the better."

"Montalvo seems like a competent medic," Sandoval observed. "She could come with us."

Ashe snorted, and Sandoval judged it best to back down. Sweeping the woods one more time with her binoculars, she put them away, then shifted her weapons belt into a more comfortable position. "The riders seem to have gone," Sandoval told Lujan. "What's your opinion, Corporal?"

"I agree, Ma'am. They wouldn't have taken their horses down to the river in the darkness, and there's no sign of a camp close to the road. I think it's safe to assume they rode on to the pass last night."

"My thoughts exactly." She stood up slowly, still uneasy about taking Ashe into danger. But the doctor refused to be left behind.

"Come along then," she said to Ashe.

* * * * *

The tracks of Lau's flight through the woods were easy to follow, Sandoval noted. Branches were broken, and the dirt trail bore a great variety of footprints. Looking down at the prints made by booted feet, she felt a cold, hard anger grow inside her. The men who made the prints, whether blood sellers, bandits, or adventurers, were not the real enemy. Nor the Red Death. The real enemy was whoever had done this to them — her troopers, Ashe, Hart, and the others — whoever had turned back the clock and pushed them backwards into barbarism. The people who had sent Valentin were the real enemy — the people who now wanted to befriend them.

237

Somewhere, she thought, somewhere there must be others who think like I do, who realize what's happening. But how to contact them? And was it too late to resist? She thought of Hart's radio, and wondered where to start. Perhaps the people at Sanctuary had some answers. But that was a project for the future. Plucking a torn scrap of gray cloth from a low-hanging branch, she examined it critically. It was stained a rusty brown.

"Blood," observed Ashe, peering over Sandoval's shoulder. "Here, too," she said, pointing to the ground just ahead of them. "This must be where Lau was shot. And Irena."

Sandoval looked around. "In that case, the body should be close by."

"Over here!" called Lujan from a little farther up the trail.

Sandoval walked slowly toward the sound of Lujan's voice, knowing what she would find before she got there.

Lujan stood in a little clearing, Irena in a heap at her feet. "She's dead, Captain," Lujan said. "She's been dead for hours. Lau doesn't need to feel bad that she ran away and left her."

Ashe knelt to examine Irena, turning the body over and, with difficulty, extracting the short metal arrow. She peered at it in evident interest. "This probably killed her at once." Tossing the arrow into the bushes, she stood up. "We're not as safe as we assumed," she said quietly.

"So it seems," Sandoval agreed. However, the knowledge neither depressed nor intimidated her. Last night, she had had a moment of grief, of longing for the peace she thought she had found. But sometime during the night she had understood. This valley was not Sanctuary, although it was a place of safety, a place to which she had been led by her vision. It was simply somewhere to rest. To heal. But it was not the end of their journey. Realizing this, she had immediately begun to plan, and, catching herself doing so, she had chuckled. Once a leader, always a leader. Perhaps it had been the salutary effect of the voices from Sanctuary but she had awakened this morning filled with resolve. And filled with another, unfamiliar emotion too. Hope.

"Corporal Lujan, you may take Irena back to the valley," she said. "Tell the others we'll be along shortly."

"Yes, Ma'am," Lujan said, bending to lift Irena into her arms.

Sandoval and Ashe stepped off the trail to let Lujan pass, and when they were alone, Sandoval turned to the physician. "Irena found her sanctuary," she remarked, "but what about yours?"

"Mine?" Ashe asked, clearly puzzled.

"I'm assuming you'll want to go to Yuma," Sandoval said. "I've heard you talk of it. Apparently there's a viable MedCenter there."

"No," Ashe answered at once. "Not Yuma."

Sandoval was surprised. "Where then?"

"Someplace where I can work in safety," Ashe said, sounding definite. "Who's to say that the BioStrike Forces won't kidnap me from my bed in Yuma one night? No, I want to . . . disappear. And take my knowledge with me. Sanctuary seems as good a destination as any. Then, once I feel safe, I want to begin work again. I can replicate my success with the vaccine." She tapped her head. "The knowledge is here."

Sandoval was skeptical. "But you'll need a medical facility. A hospital. Or a research institute. I doubt there's one left standing in all of California."

"I don't need very much," Ashe said. "Equipment can be bought. Or made. Or stolen. I know exactly what's required."

"You certainly seem to," Sandoval said in amazement. "But what would you do with the vaccine once you've produced it? The problems —"

Ashe waved a hand, cutting off Sandoval's objections. "What would I do with it? I'd give it away, of course."

"Of course," Sandoval said drily. "And I'm certain you've thought about the mechanics. Things like communication. Distribution."

"I've thought about them."

"Well?"

"Well what?" Ashe said truculently.

"Well, how would you let people know about the vaccine? Valentin's masters have done a pretty good job of suppressing its existence so far."

Sandoval heard Ashe take a deep breath. "I'd use Sanctuary's radio network."

Sandoval said nothing for a moment, thinking. Well, why not? It might just work. "That's an ambitious plan," she said at last.

Ashe shrugged. "Do you have a better one in mind?"

"No," Sandoval had to admit, "I don't."

"Well then, it's settled," Ashe said. "Once Hart finds out exactly where we're going — and we've had time to let our broken bones set — we can get started. We can't delay, though. I'd say we need to leave by summer. That gives us two months at best."

Sandoval shook her head. Could she lead this ragtag band of refugees safely through California to the north coast? She began to think of the dozens of things that could go wrong and closed her eyes, overwhelmed.

"Having doubts already, Captain?"

"Some," Sandoval admitted.

"Good," Ashe said. "We can trade misgivings if you like. But maybe we can wait until tomorrow. Right now, we should get back to the valley, bury Irena, have a decent meal, and start catching up on our sleep."

"That sounds like a good idea," Sandoval said.

"It's a prescription, not a suggestion," Ashe said testily. "If you're going to be any good to us, you're going to have to take care of yourself. Eat. Get more rest."

Sandoval was about to disagree with Ashe, to assert her authority, to remind her who was in charge here after all, when she suddenly changed her mind. Perhaps the Doctor was right. A little rest wouldn't hurt at all. Even though, strictly speaking, she didn't need it. Still . . .

"If we're to be at all useful we have to prepare," Ashe said. "I have a vaccination program to organize — we need to know that we no longer have the Red Death to fear. And above all, we need to regain our strength. It's as though we've been given a reprieve, isn't it? Another chance. We can rest here. Grow strong again. Heal."

A reprieve, another chance? Sandoval liked those

ideas. Perhaps the skills she and her women had learned in the BioStrike Forces — good, solid military virtues — could be put to work in a better, more productive cause. Reaching Sanctuary, for instance. And after that? Tempting though the prospect was, she refused to speculate.

"What you say makes sense," she told Ashe with a smile. "But then, it usually does. So it's rest you prescribe, is it? Well, let's go back to the valley and begin. After all, isn't that what sanctuaries are for?"

A few of the publications of
THE NAIAD PRESS, INC.
P.O. Box 10543 ● **Tallahassee, Florida 32302**
Phone (904) 539-5965
Mail orders welcome. Please include 15% postage.

IN THE BLOOD by Lauren Wright Douglas. 252 pp. Lesbian
science fiction adventure fantasy   ISBN 0-941483-22-3 $8.95

THE BEE'S KISS by Shirley Verel. 216 pp. Delicate, delicious
romance.   ISBN 0-941483-36-3   8.95

RAGING MOTHER MOUNTAIN by Pat Emmerson. 264 pp.
Furosa Firechild's adventures in Wonderland. ISBN 0-941483-35-5   8.95

IN EVERY PORT by Karin Kallmaker. 228 pp. Jessica's sexy,
adventuresome travels.   ISBN 0-941483-37-7   8.95

OF LOVE AND GLORY by Evelyn Kennedy. 192 pp. Exciting
WWII romance.   ISBN 0-941483-32-0   8.95

CLICKING STONES by Nancy Tyler Glenn. 288 pp. Love
transcending time.   ISBN 0-941483-31-2   8.95

SURVIVING SISTERS by Gail Pass. 252 pp. Powerful love
story.   ISBN 0-941483-16-9   8.95

SOUTH OF THE LINE by Catherine Ennis. 216 pp. Civil War
adventure.   ISBN 0-941483-29-0   8.95

WOMAN PLUS WOMAN by Dolores Klaich. 300 pp. Supurb
Lesbian overview.   ISBN 0-941483-28-2   9.95

SLOW DANCING AT MISS POLLY'S by Sheila Ortiz Taylor.
96 pp. Lesbian Poetry   ISBN 0-941483-30-4   7.95

DOUBLE DAUGHTER by Vicki P. McConnell. 216 pp. A Nyla
Wade Mystery, third in the series.   ISBN 0-941483-26-6   8.95

HEAVY GILT by Delores Klaich. 192 pp. Lesbian detective/
disappearing homophobes/upper class gay society.
          ISBN 0-941483-25-8   8.95

THE FINER GRAIN by Denise Ohio. 216 pp. Brilliant young
college lesbian novel.   ISBN 0-941483-11-8   8.95

THE AMAZON TRAIL by Lee Lynch. 216 pp. Life, travel & lore
of famous lesbian author.   ISBN 0-941483-27-4   8.95

HIGH CONTRAST by Jessie Lattimore. 264 pp. Women of the
Crystal Palace.   ISBN 0-941483-17-7   8.95

OCTOBER OBSESSION by Meredith More. Josie's rich, secret
Lesbian life.   ISBN 0-941483-18-5   8.95

LESBIAN CROSSROADS by Ruth Baetz. 276 pp. Contemporary
Lesbian lives.   ISBN 0-941483-21-5   9.95

BEFORE STONEWALL: THE MAKING OF A GAY AND
LESBIAN COMMUNITY by Andrea Weiss & Greta Schiller.
96 pp., 25 illus.   ISBN 0-941483-20-7   7.95

WE WALK THE BACK OF THE TIGER by Patricia A. Murphy.
192 pp. Romantic Lesbian novel/beginning women's movement.
                                           ISBN 0-941483-13-4   8.95

SUNDAY'S CHILD by Joyce Bright. 216 pp. Lesbian athletics, at
last the novel about sports.   ISBN 0-941483-12-6   8.95

OSTEN'S BAY by Zenobia N. Vole. 204 pp. Sizzling adventure
romance set on Bonaire.   ISBN 0-941483-15-0   8.95

LESSONS IN MURDER by Claire McNab. 216 pp. 1st in a stylish
mystery series.   ISBN 0-941483-14-2   8.95

YELLOWTHROAT by Penny Hayes. 240 pp. Margarita, bandit,
kidnaps Julia.   ISBN 0-941483-10-X   8.95

SAPPHISTRY: THE BOOK OF LESBIAN SEXUALITY by
Pat Califia. 3d edition, revised. 208 pp.   ISBN 0-941483-24-X   8.95

CHERISHED LOVE by Evelyn Kennedy. 192 pp. Erotic
Lesbian love story.   ISBN 0-941483-08-8   8.95

LAST SEPTEMBER by Helen R. Hull. 208 pp. Six stories & a
glorious novella.   ISBN 0-941483-09-6   8.95

THE SECRET IN THE BIRD by Camarin Grae. 312 pp. Striking,
psychological suspense novel.   ISBN 0-941483-05-3   8.95

TO THE LIGHTNING by Catherine Ennis. 208 pp. Romantic
Lesbian 'Robinson Crusoe' adventure.   ISBN 0-941483-06-1   8.95

THE OTHER SIDE OF VENUS by Shirley Verel. 224 pp.
Luminous, romantic love story.   ISBN 0-941483-07-X   8.95

DREAMS AND SWORDS by Katherine V. Forrest. 192 pp.
Romantic, erotic, imaginative stories.   ISBN 0-941483-03-7   8.95

MEMORY BOARD by Jane Rule. 336 pp. Memorable novel
about an aging Lesbian couple.   ISBN 0-941483-02-9   8.95

THE ALWAYS ANONYMOUS BEAST by Lauren Wright
Douglas. 224 pp. A Caitlin Reese mystery. First in a series.
                                           ISBN 0-941483-04-5   8.95

SEARCHING FOR SPRING by Patricia A. Murphy. 224 pp.
Novel about the recovery of love.   ISBN 0-941483-00-2   8.95

DUSTY'S QUEEN OF HEARTS DINER by Lee Lynch. 240 pp.
Romantic blue-collar novel.   ISBN 0-941483-01-0   8.95

PARENTS MATTER by Ann Muller. 240 pp. Parents'
relationships with Lesbian daughters and gay sons.
                                           ISBN 0-930044-91-6   9.95

THE PEARLS by Shelley Smith. 176 pp. Passion and fun in
the Caribbean sun.   ISBN 0-930044-93-2   7.95

MAGDALENA by Sarah Aldridge. 352 pp. Epic Lesbian novel
set on three continents.   ISBN 0-930044-99-1   8.95

THE BLACK AND WHITE OF IT by Ann Allen Shockley.
144 pp. Short stories.   ISBN 0-930044-96-7   7.95

SAY JESUS AND COME TO ME by Ann Allen Shockley. 288
pp. Contemporary romance.   ISBN 0-930044-98-3   8.95

LOVING HER by Ann Allen Shockley. 192 pp. Romantic love
story.   ISBN 0-930044-97-5   7.95

MURDER AT THE NIGHTWOOD BAR by Katherine V.
Forrest. 240 pp. A Kate Delafield mystery. Second in a series.
                                              ISBN 0-930044-92-4   8.95

ZOE'S BOOK by Gail Pass. 224 pp. Passionate, obsessive love
story.   ISBN 0-930044-95-9   7.95

WINGED DANCER by Camarin Grae. 228 pp. Erotic Lesbian
adventure story.   ISBN 0-930044-88-6   8.95

PAZ by Camarin Grae. 336 pp. Romantic Lesbian adventurer
with the power to change the world.   ISBN 0-930044-89-4   8.95

SOUL SNATCHER by Camarin Grae. 224 pp. A puzzle, an
adventure, a mystery — Lesbian romance.   ISBN 0-930044-90-8   8.95

THE LOVE OF GOOD WOMEN by Isabel Miller. 224 pp.
Long-awaited new novel by the author of the beloved *Patience
and Sarah.*   ISBN 0-930044-81-9   8.95

THE HOUSE AT PELHAM FALLS by Brenda Weathers. 240
pp. Suspenseful Lesbian ghost story.   ISBN 0-930044-79-7   7.95

HOME IN YOUR HANDS by Lee Lynch. 240 pp. More stories
from the author of *Old Dyke Tales.*   ISBN 0-930044-80-0   7.95

EACH HAND A MAP by Anita Skeen. 112 pp. Real-life poems
that touch us all.   ISBN 0-930044-82-7   6.95

SURPLUS by Sylvia Stevenson. 342 pp. A classic early Lesbian
novel.   ISBN 0-930044-78-9   7.95

PEMBROKE PARK by Michelle Martin. 256 pp. Derring-do
and daring romance in Regency England.   ISBN 0-930044-77-0   7.95

THE LONG TRAIL by Penny Hayes. 248 pp. Vivid adventures
of two women in love in the old west.   ISBN 0-930044-76-2   8.95

HORIZON OF THE HEART by Shelley Smith. 192 pp. Hot
romance in summertime New England.   ISBN 0-930044-75-4   7.95

AN EMERGENCE OF GREEN by Katherine V. Forrest. 288
pp. Powerful novel of sexual discovery.   ISBN 0-930044-69-X   8.95

THE LESBIAN PERIODICALS INDEX edited by Claire
Potter. 432 pp. Author & subject index.   ISBN 0-930044-74-6   29.95

DESERT OF THE HEART by Jane Rule. 224 pp. A classic;
basis for the movie *Desert Hearts.*   ISBN 0-930044-73-8   7.95

SPRING FORWARD/FALL BACK by Sheila Ortiz Taylor.
288 pp. Literary novel of timeless love.   ISBN 0-930044-70-3   7.95

FOR KEEPS by Elisabeth Nonas. 144 pp. Contemporary novel
about losing and finding love.   ISBN 0-930044-71-1   7.95

TORCHLIGHT TO VALHALLA by Gale Wilhelm. 128 pp.
Classic novel by a great Lesbian writer.   ISBN 0-930044-68-1   7.95

LESBIAN NUNS: BREAKING SILENCE edited by Rosemary
Curb and Nancy Manahan. 432 pp. Unprecedented autobiographies
of religious life.   ISBN 0-930044-62-2   9.95

THE SWASHBUCKLER by Lee Lynch. 288 pp. Colorful novel
set in Greenwich Village in the sixties.   ISBN 0-930044-66-5   8.95

MISFORTUNE'S FRIEND by Sarah Aldridge. 320 pp. Historical Lesbian novel set on two continents.   ISBN 0-930044-67-3   7.95

A STUDIO OF ONE'S OWN by Ann Stokes. Edited by
Dolores Klaich. 128 pp. Autobiography.   ISBN 0-930044-64-9   7.95

SEX VARIANT WOMEN IN LITERATURE by Jeannette
Howard Foster. 448 pp. Literary history.   ISBN 0-930044-65-7   8.95

A HOT-EYED MODERATE by Jane Rule. 252 pp. Hard-hitting
essays on gay life; writing; art.   ISBN 0-930044-57-6   7.95

INLAND PASSAGE AND OTHER STORIES by Jane Rule.
288 pp. Wide-ranging new collection.   ISBN 0-930044-56-8   7.95

WE TOO ARE DRIFTING by Gale Wilhelm. 128 pp. Timeless
Lesbian novel, a masterpiece.   ISBN 0-930044-61-4   6.95

AMATEUR CITY by Katherine V. Forrest. 224 pp. A Kate
Delafield mystery. First in a series.   ISBN 0-930044-55-X   7.95

THE SOPHIE HOROWITZ STORY by Sarah Schulman. 176
pp. Engaging novel of madcap intrigue.   ISBN 0-930044-54-1   7.95

THE BURNTON WIDOWS by Vickie P. McConnell. 272 pp. A
Nyla Wade mystery, second in the series.   ISBN 0-930044-52-5   7.95

OLD DYKE TALES by Lee Lynch. 224 pp. Extraordinary
stories of our diverse Lesbian lives.   ISBN 0-930044-51-7   8.95

DAUGHTERS OF A CORAL DAWN by Katherine V. Forrest.
240 pp. Novel set in a Lesbian new world.   ISBN 0-930044-50-9   7.95

THE PRICE OF SALT by Claire Morgan. 288 pp. A milestone
novel, a beloved classic.   ISBN 0-930044-49-5   8.95

AGAINST THE SEASON by Jane Rule. 224 pp. Luminous,
complex novel of interrelationships.   ISBN 0-930044-48-7   8.95

These are just a few of the many Naiad Press titles — we are the oldest and largest lesbian/feminist publishing company in the world. Please request a complete catalog. We offer personal service; we encourage and welcome direct mail orders from individuals who have limited access to bookstores carrying our publications.